Blake acts on instinct when he steals a dragon egg from his boss. He's never done anything that stupid, and now, he's in trouble, both with humans and dragons.

Especially with the dragon that captures him.

But Orran is not merely a dragon. He's also a beautiful man, and Blake is stuck with him — and with a baby dragon after the egg hatches.

Blake's boss isn't done with him or with the baby, which means Blake has to gain Orran's trust and convince him to take him with him. He has nothing to go back to in the city except death if his boss catches him. Death might still find him if he leaves with Orran, but he has nothing to lose.

Or does he?

Blue Fire
Copyright © 2020 Catherine Lievens
ISBN: 978-1-4874-2996-6
Cover art by Angela Waters

Published by eXtasy Books Inc or
Devine Destinies, an imprint of eXtasy Books Inc

Look for us online at:
www.eXtasybooks.com or www.devinedestinies.com

Blue Fire
Ogorth Clan 1

By

Catherine Lievens

CHAPTER ONE

Orran opened one eye when he heard the ruckus outside his bedroom. He huffed, smoke coming out of his nose. He was tempted to go to the door to yell at the people running outside, but he knew there had to be a good reason for them to make so much noise. He wasn't sure he wanted to find out, but since he was one of the queen's guards, he probably should.

He stretched, his wings expanding. Then he shook his head and lumbered toward the door. Hearing someone pound on it made him jump, and he scowled at it. He grumbled, and the door opened.

One of the guards was standing on the other side of it, in his human form. Orran arched a brow at him, and the man shook his head. "It's the queen's egg. It's gone."

Orran jerked back. Gone? The queen's egg was gone? How was that possible? He glared at the guard again, hating that the man was in his human form. It meant they couldn't communicate, and if Orran had to go after the thief, he needed to know everything there was to know, but he also probably needed to be in his dragon form.

He shifted. "What happened?" he asked.

"No one knows."

"Who sent you here?"

"The queen."

Orran nodded. "She wants to see me?"

"She does. She told me to get you."

"Good. I'm heading her way." Orran paused, then looked

at the man again. "You need to stay in your dragon form." He didn't understand why so many of the younger dragons enjoyed being in their human form. He couldn't say he hated it, but being a dragon felt so much more natural to him.

The man's cheeks flushed. "I will. I apologize."

Orran shook his head. "There's nothing to apologize for. You can be in this form as much as you want on your own time, but you need to be a dragon when working. The queen needs you to be."

The man nodded, and Orran wasn't sure whether or not he'd gotten through to him, but it didn't matter, especially not right now.

He shifted again, then headed toward the center of the hallway, where the ceiling was open.

Once there, he took flight, heading toward the queen's tower. She was the only one who lived there, along with her offspring, which for now was her only egg. Orran didn't understand how someone had managed to get in there. It had to have been a dragon, right? It was the only thing that made sense. Humans might try to steal eggs and kill dragons, but there was no way they would have been able to get into the palace. It just wasn't possible.

Yet Orran couldn't think of one dragon who would tempt fate and do something like this. The queen was the most important person in the palace. She was the leader of their small cluster, and she protected her dragons from humans and rival clusters. Who would want to do something like that to her, to betray her this way? Orran didn't understand. He didn't much care, either. Whoever had the egg would pay, and that was all that mattered.

When he got to the queen's quarters, the place was a flurry of activity. Dragons flew in and out of her rooms, mostly ignoring Orran. He didn't stop to talk to any of them. He realized they were trying to help, but he doubted the egg was anywhere close. Whoever had taken it had run away with it.

The queen was in her throne room, pacing its length, her tail swishing nervously. Orran had to step back to avoid being hit in the head, and the queen jumped when she noticed him. *Orran. Thank God.*

Orran blinked. He wasn't used to the queen talking to him that way. He wouldn't say they were friends, but they were fairly close, since she'd personally chosen him to guide her team of Queen's Guard. His position was official, which was why hearing her talking that informally to him was strange.

He bowed his head. *My queen?*

She stopped in front of him. *It's gone. My egg.*

That's what I was told. Do you know what happened?

She shook her head. *I have no idea. I couldn't sleep, so I went to visit it, and when I got there, the nest was empty. I knew I should have kept it in my bedroom.*

It's not tradition.

She snorted smoke. *Tradition? Who cares about tradition? If I never get it back . . .*

She didn't have to say it. Orran knew what she was saying.

Dragons weren't very fertile. They could only get impregnated once every few years, and as the queen, she needed to produce an heir. That was what she'd done, except that now, the heir was gone.

Orran straightened. *What can I do?* he asked. He had no doubt she had something specific in mind, since she'd called for him.

The queen sucked in a breath. *I need you to go after whoever took the egg. I need you to take it back.*

Do you have any idea who did this?

She shook her head. *Not yet, but I asked one of your team members to check the cameras.*

Orran nodded. Sometimes, it was still weird to think they were using human things to keep an eye on the palace, but humans could be useful, almost as much as they could be cruel. The queen had installed cameras all over the palace, but especially at the entrances, so they would be able to see anyone who had come in and gone out. If the egg was outside of the palace, they would know who had taken it, and Orran would be able to go after them. He hoped it had been a dragon and that they were still in the palace, but the thief could have come from any of the close by clusters, and if that was the case, it would make the situation more complicated.

The queen huffed again. *Take some of the guards from the Queen's Guard with you. I don't want people to find out what happened, and I trust all of you.*

They couldn't afford for the news to get out. Someone might use the situation to their advantage and try to push her off the throne. They couldn't allow that to happen, though. The queen was a good leader, and Orran hoped she would stay queen for a long time. *I'll let you know as soon as I know something.*

Check the cameras, too. You need to know who has my baby.

I'll go as soon as I've picked my team.

She nodded, then hesitated. *I don't need to tell you how important it this that you recover the egg.*

Orran's heart squeezed. *Of course not. I'll do my best. We all will.*

She nodded. They both knew that eventually, she might have another egg, but it wouldn't be for a few years, and in the meantime, her throne would be in danger. It was the last thing they needed. They also shouldn't think about this right now, though. Orran had work to do, and he needed to do it now.

He bowed his head again, then moved toward the door. He already had a few people for his team in mind, and the first of those people was Morven. Morven was his best friend, and he would keep his mouth shut. He would also be Orran's second, just like he was when it came to the Queen's Guard. Together, they would get the egg back. Orran wasn't looking forward to leaving part of the Guard behind, but the queen had to be protected, now more than ever.

Orran headed toward the security room. The hallways were mostly empty, and a tense silence pressed against him. He shifted when he got to the room because of how small the commands to the screens were. Then he walked in.

Orran waited a moment, long enough to assess who was in the room and what was happening, then he cleared his throat. Everyone turned to look at him. There were too many people there, people who had nothing to do with the situation, and they knew it. He arched a brow at them, and they scattered, sheepish. He hoped no one would flap their mouths, but just in case, he made a mental note to tell the Guard who would be in charge while he was gone to make sure they didn't talk.

Morven stayed, looking amused even though he was in his dragon form, stuck in a corner. The light glinted on his leathery skin, and he chuckled. Since he was there, Orran wanted to talk to him. He looked at the palace guard who operated the screens. "Show me the nest room. I want to see the entire night, but start with looking for the thieves." Then he shifted and turned his attention to Morven.

That went well, Morven said.

I need people to be focused, and if they shouldn't be here, they need to go, Orran answered.

Of course. What do you need?

The queen assigned me the task of finding her egg. She told me to put a team together, and I want you to be my second.

Morven didn't even look surprised. *Tell me.*

Orran explained the situation. He didn't know what would happen, but he already felt better with his best friend by his side. It wouldn't be easy, but he wasn't doing this alone. *Do you already know who else will be coming? How big should the team be?*

The queen asked for a small one, and we need most of the Guard to be here and protect her, just in case, so maybe another three of us?

5

Morven nodded. *I know who to pick. Octavia, Slavin, and Hogan.*

Orran agreed with him. He knew why the queen had put him in charge, but it made him uncomfortable. He was supposed to be here, at the head of the Guard, protecting her. Instead, he would probably have to leave the palace, and there was no way to know for how long. But either the palace had been breached, or they had a traitor on their hands. Orran didn't know which one it was, but he was about to find out. Whoever had the egg, he feared the worst. They needed to act now before everything was lost.

"Orran?" the guard at the screens said.

Orran shifted back. "Who?" he asked.

The guard turned the screen so Orran could see what was playing on it. "Humans."

Orran sucked in a breath. "You're sure?"

"A hundred percent. Look at the screen."

Orran did. He didn't know how they'd managed to get in, and it wasn't his job to find out. The palace guards would. *His* job was to get to the egg, and that was what he would do.

He looked at Morven and nodded. "Let's go. We need to get to them before they hurt the egg."

The sounds in the bar were subdued, but the clients less so. Blake was used to it, and he kept his head down and worked. His job was to serve drinks, restock the bar and wash dishes, something he was good at. But then, who wouldn't be good at washing dishes? No matter how boring the job was, he was glad for it, and he did his best not to get himself in trouble. It was hard some days, considering the clients, but he managed, and that was what mattered.

He rinsed another glass and looked up. The people were rowdy, but it was familiar and comforting. His life's dream hadn't been to work in a bar, but it was what it was. The one thing he hated was that he was sure his boss was involved in shady stuff. He had disliked the man when he'd first met him, and that opinion hadn't changed. Still, this was a good job and decently paid, even though he'd been surprised in the beginning to find out how much money he would make. He supposed the boss was also buying his silence, asking him to close an eye to whatever illegal stuff he had going on. As long as no one got hurt, Blake was more than happy to do just that. He wasn't about to stick his nose into stuff that wasn't his business, not unless he needed to.

The noise was finally winding down, the bar about to close for the night. Blake relaxed, slid another beer toward one of their regulars, then went back to his cleaning. That was when the bar door opened.

Blake looked up, ready to tell the customers they were about to close, but he stopped the words from leaving his lips when he saw who it was.

He didn't know the group of men standing there. He'd never met them, and if he'd seen them in a dark alley, he would have turned around and left. He wasn't in a dark alley, though. He was in a bar, and even though it wasn't well lit, he knew he couldn't ignore them.

He cleared his throat. "What can I help you with?" he asked as he dried his hands with a towel.

One of the men stepped forward. Another just looked around, and one of them was holding a bag that looked heavy and as though a ball was inside it. "We're here to see the owner."

Blake nodded. He wasn't surprised. "He's in the back. You know the way?"

The man nodded, gestured at the four men behind him, and headed toward the back. He did know where he needed to go, which told Blake this wasn't the first time the man had dealt with his boss.

Blake shook his head. It wasn't his business — it didn't matter how worried he was. As long as he stayed out of it, he would be okay.

He went back to his glasses, but he couldn't help but wonder what was happening. He decided to text his brother. That would help him take his mind off things.

Blake: *You'll never believe what just happened.*

The three dots moved on the screen, telling him his brother was answering.

Sheldon: *You created a new cocktail?*

Blake rolled his eyes. *I already told you that's not the kind of barman I am or the kind of bar this is.*

Sheldon: *Right. What happened, then? Did your boss finally help you clean up?*

That was never going to happen, either. *Of course not. You know him.*

Sheldon: *Better than I ever wanted to know him, yes. Are you going to tell me what happened, then?*

Blake: *Not sure. A group of weird guys came in and wanted to see him. I'm pretty sure that whatever's happening is not legal.*

There was a pause, and Blake watched the dots. They moved, then stopped, then started moving again. Sheldon was obviously thinking about what to write.

Their relationship was a weird one, so Blake understood why his brother was being careful. He didn't want to push Blake away, but then, Blake didn't want to be pushed away. Sheldon was the only family Blake had left, and he wasn't going to do anything to put their relationship in jeopardy.

Sheldon: *Do you need to leave?*

Blake: *I'm not leaving. Those people had nothing to do with me. I told you, they went in the back.*

Sheldon: *We both know that whatever is happening in the back isn't legal. You shouldn't be working there, Blake.*

That, too, was a spot of contention between them. Blake had taken the job because he *needed* a job. Sheldon hadn't been happy about it. He'd suggested that he could provide for Blake until Blake found something better, but Blake hadn't wanted him to. The last thing he needed was for his family to think he was a freeloader because his brother was paying for him. They refused to talk to Blake and had made it clear that he wasn't welcome in the family anymore, but they wouldn't miss the chance to tell Sheldon just how wrong he was for sticking with Blake.

Blake: *I'll be fine. I'm staying out of trouble, I promise. I'm going nowhere near the back. He doesn't need me there, and he was adamant that he wanted me to keep my nose out of things. That's what I'm going to do.*

Sheldon: *Are you sure? Because you're not known for keeping your nose out of things.*

Blake grimaced. Okay, so maybe he was curious. That didn't mean he was reckless.

Blake: *Don't worry. I promise I'll be okay.*

The sound of voices coming from the back made him look up. Someone was laughing, and when the group stepped back into the main room, Blake's boss was with them. He was the one laughing, which was a surprise, because he never even smiled, and when he looked up, he gestured at Blake. "Serve us the good stuff, will you?"

Blake nodded and jumped to obey. He wasn't about to ask what was happening, but Hans and his friends were celebrating. What, Blake didn't know, and he didn't care. It was none of his business.

He slid the drinks over the bar and watched as Hans drank one down, then asked for another. He stayed silent as he worked, but his mind was working. Why was his boss so happy?

"Shit. I forgot my phone on my desk," Hans said.

He tried hopping off the stool he was sitting on and almost fell on his face, which made everyone laugh. If Blake had to guess, these were far from being his first drinks tonight. Hans sat back down, rubbing the back of his neck. "Well, that's not going to happen." He looked at Blake. "Go grab my phone. It's on my desk."

Blake blinked. He'd never been allowed in the office. "Are you sure?" he asked.

"Of course I'm sure," Hans snapped. "I wouldn't be asking otherwise. Go get my phone, boy."

Blake resisted the urge to roll his eyes. *Boy?* Really? He was twenty-seven, for fuck's sake. He put down his towel and headed toward the back of the bar. He'd never been in the office, not even when he'd been hired. He knew where it was, but he wasn't allowed inside.

Until today.

He had no idea what was happening, but it had to be big to make his boss drink so much that he'd ordered him to fetch the phone.

Blake pushed open the office door and peered in. He could see the desk and the phone, and he made a beeline for it. He noticed that the closet door was open as he turned to go back to the bar, and he hesitated. He shouldn't be doing this. It wasn't any of his business, and it was probably dangerous. But like Sheldon had said, he was curious, and he was dying to find out what was happening. He knew it had to be illegal. As far as he knew, his boss had never hurt anyone, but what if he was this time? It wouldn't surprise Blake. Hans didn't have feelings, and he wouldn't hesitate to hurt people as long as it made money. If that was the case here, Blake wanted to know. He wanted to get out of here before things could get worse, and he wanted to help.

He cautiously opened the partially closed door. He half expected something or someone to jump him, but everything was quiet, and nothing moved. It could be nothing. It could be only coats or whatever. Blake had to check, though. He'd come too far not to. He reached for the light switch and flipped it.

It wasn't coats. He sucked in a breath when he saw the egg resting on a bundled coat.

Where had his boss found a dragon egg? Blake was in awe for a second. Then he started to panic. *Shit.* His boss had a dragon egg. Blake could too easily imagine what was going to happen to the poor dragon inside the egg. Either it would be killed as soon as it came out of the egg, or it would be raised in cruelty and pain. His body would be harvested for skin, teeth, and everything else people could sell on the black market. It would wish it was dead, if it could do such a thing.

If there was one thing Blake hated about humanity, it was the way they treated animals, and dragons weren't any different.

He hesitated. He knew he would get in trouble if he tried to help, but he couldn't ignore the egg. He didn't have it in him. It wasn't his job, far from it, but he needed to keep the egg safe. He couldn't leave it here, not when he could guess what would happen to it.

So, even though he knew it was probably the worst thing he could do, he took the egg and carefully lifted it until it was level with his face. He had no clue what he was doing, but there was a baby inside the egg, and he found himself saying, "I'll do everything I can to keep you safe. I promise." He didn't know if the dragon could hear him, but he wanted to soothe it and reassure it.

He knew he only had a few moments before his boss realized he was gone and understood what was happening. Instead of going back to the front of the bar, he dumped the cell back on the desk and headed toward the back door. That was the door through which he came in and left every day, so he knew where he was going. He stepped into the alley in the back and looked around, his heart racing.

He should have known Hans had noticed something was

off already. The group of men who'd entered the bar earlier were waiting for him at the entrance of the alley. They looked ready to kill him, and Blake had no doubt that was what would happen.

As soon as they got the egg back.

He held his breath, wondering what was about to happen. Hans stepped closer, shaking his head. "I should have known better than to send you to my office," he said.

Blake hugged the egg close to his chest. "What will you do with it?" he asked.

"None of your business. You should have kept your nose out of my closet."

Blake should have. Now, the dragon would be tortured and killed, while Blake would be killed. What he'd done hadn't changed anything.

The wind picked up, and all of them looked toward the sky. Blake's eyes widened when he saw dragons coming closer, ready to land.

"Shit," someone yelled. A few of the people who were standing with his boss tried to run away, but one of the dragons landed at the alley entrance, boxing them in.

They were in trouble.

That was when Hans tried to take the egg. Blake had no idea what was happening, but he did know he couldn't allow that to happen, so he clung onto it. It wasn't easy, not when his boss kicked him in the balls. He folded in half and let the egg go. Hans tried to catch it, but he stumbled, and the egg fell to the ground.

Blake's eyes widened, and he scrambled to get the egg. Had he just killed the baby inside it?

Orran saw the egg drop to the ground. He roared, making several of the humans jump, including the one who had been holding the egg. Then he threw himself toward it. He needed to get to the egg. He needed to get it back.

It wasn't that easy. Everyone around him was fighting. The humans were afraid of dragons, but that didn't mean they would stop. If anything, having so many dragons there at once, especially adult ones, could turn to their advantage if they managed to kill even one of them. The survivors would be able to sell off the fallen's body in pieces.

Orran wouldn't allow that to happen.

When two humans rushed toward him, he swiped his tail at them and threw them against the closest wall. One of them didn't get up. The other did, but it seemed like he wasn't going to come for Orran again. Instead, he eyed the opening of the alley and tried to sneak out that way, but Octavia thumped her tail right in front of him and roared in his face.

Orran turned his attention back to the egg. He leaned down to grab it with one of his paws, but someone got there before he did.

The same human who had been holding it earlier grabbed it with both his hands and pulled it against his chest.

Orran roared. The sound made everything vibrate around them. Human cities weren't made for dragons, and the alley was tiny, so small that Orran would have trouble getting back into the air. He didn't care right now, though. He stood in front of the human and lowered his head to look him in the eyes. He wanted to tear the human's head off, but he knew better. He needed to make sure the humans hadn't hurt the egg.

The human stayed where he was. His eyes were wide and his face ashen, and he was looking around the alley, no doubt trying to find a way to escape. He couldn't, though.

Orran wouldn't allow him to run away. He needed to get the egg back, but when he reached for it again, the human shook his head and took a step sideways, as if trying to walk around Orran.

Orran huffed. He didn't have time for this. The last thing he wanted was to shift. Humans weren't aware that dragons weren't merely animals, and Orran didn't want any of them to find out, but it seemed this was where the situation was going. He needed to be fast, though, so only this human would see him.

He looked around. All the humans were busy fighting, so he doubted they would notice if he shifted. The pros outweighed the cons, no matter how much he disliked this, so he decided it was the best thing he could do.

He shifted. He hadn't thought it possible, but the human's eyes went even wider. He looked Orran up and down, opened his mouth, and *croaked*.

Orran ignored him and reached out. "Give me the egg," he said.

That seemed to get the human's attention again. He shook his head, then took a step back. "Don't touch it."

"I don't care what you intended to do with it. It doesn't belong to you."

The human's expression shifted.

Unfortunately, Orran wasn't used to being with humans, and he had no idea what it meant.

"I know it doesn't belong to me," the human said. "How do I know it belongs to you, though?"

Orran snorted. "I'm a dragon. You *know* it belongs to me."

The human looked down at the egg. "So? Even if you're a dragon, I can't know that it's your egg. How am I supposed to make sure of that? Besides, you're a guy."

Orran had no idea what that had to do with anything. "I'll kill you," he said, his voice dark and steady. "You had no right to steal the egg. You have no right to kill and hurt us and to invade our home."

The human shook his head frantically. "You don't

understand. I didn't steal the egg. I was trying to rescue it from my boss."

"Nice try, but as far as I can see, you're the one holding it. You're the one keeping it away from me. You *have* to give it to me."

Things weren't going anywhere. Orran waited, but the human didn't seem to change his mind. "I'm sorry. I can't give it to you. I can't be sure it really is your egg, and after what just happened, I'm not going to trust anyone, not even you," the human said.

Orran shifted back. If he couldn't talk sense into the human, maybe he would be able to scare him.

The human squeaked when Orran lowered his head so close to him that he could feel the human's breath on his snout. There was nowhere for him to go. His back was against the wall, and they were at the end of the alley, so he couldn't sneak away. They could stay here forever, or at least until the human gave Orran the egg. The human, on the other hand, was going to want to leave eventually. Either that, or he'd faint. He looked like he might be about to.

Something heavy hit Orran's side, and he roared. He turned to face whatever had touched him and realized that while he and the human had been talking, more humans had appeared. The dragons had always been outnumbered, but it hadn't mattered because they were dragons. Now, though, it looked like it might become a problem.

Orran couldn't lose the egg, and he wasn't about to leave any of his friends in the humans' hands. He knew what would be done to them if that happened, and death was preferable to that. He turned toward the human again, but the man still looked resolute. He wouldn't give Orran the egg, and that meant that Orran would have to grab both of them. It would be faster than trying to talk the human into doing this. He could always deal with the man later — once the egg was safe.

We're leaving, he projected to the members of his team.

You have the egg? Morven asked.

Not yet, but I'll have it when we take to the air. Go, he ordered.

Then, he reached out, wrapped his paw around the human, and rose into the air.

The human screamed. The screech hurt Orran's ears, but he ignored it as he and his four team members rose as high as they could. The humans in the alley were shooting at them, trying to take them down, but it would take more than that to hurt a dragon.

And the humans had more than that. Orran's eyes widened when he saw one of them take out the biggest gun he'd ever seen. He had no idea what it could do, but he could too easily imagine. *Scatter!* He was yelling through the mind bond he shared with the other dragons.

They obeyed without protesting, and it was a good thing. The human holding the gun had started shooting, and Orran knew he was lucky to be far enough away that he wasn't hit. Even though normal bullets didn't usually hurt dragons, this looked like it would do some damage, and he couldn't allow that to happen. He finally had the egg back, albeit along with a human. He needed to get back to the palace.

What do we do? Morven asked.

Fly away. We should probably separate so they don't try to get us at the same time. We'll meet again in a few hours, once we're sure they're not following us.

Got it. See you soon.

Orran snorted to himself and flew away from the alley and from the city in which they'd found the egg. The human was wriggling in his hold, but Orran ignored it. It was easy. The human was light, but he was carrying the future of their clan, and Orran needed to be careful. He couldn't drop the human and the egg. He had no idea what he would do with a human, but he would find something.

If things came to that, he could always kill him.

CHAPTER TWO

Blake was freaking out. He was flying—*flying*. The guy, dragon, whatever, had grabbed Blake and flown away. Blake had no idea what that guy had been, but he'd been a dragon, then he'd become a guy. Blake had never known dragons could turn into humans. Of course, he'd never known a dragon, period, so he only knew what he'd read. Now, he *did* know a dragon, and that dragon could turn into a human, and they were fucking flying.

The dragon hadn't become a human like Blake. His skin hadn't been quite right in some places, and even though it had been dark, Blake had noticed that wasn't the only thing that differed, but the man had spoken with a human voice, and it had been terrifying. It still was. Blake had no idea what was happening except for the fact that he was fucking flying, and he was terrified of heights.

He screwed his eyes shut and clung to the egg he was still holding. There was nothing he could do. He was entirely in the hands—paws—of the dragon holding him. He should try to wiggle his way out, but he would plummet to his death, and obviously, that was the last thing he wanted to happen. What he wanted was to go home and hide in his bedroom, forget about all of this, especially the weird human-dragon thing, but he couldn't. He wasn't going anywhere, though, and he wouldn't let go of the egg until he was sure it was safe.

That was probably why the dragon looked like he might hate him.

Blake should have handed the egg over. It would have

made sense. It was a dragon egg, and a dragon had demanded it from him. But he felt responsible for the egg. He'd been the one to rescue it, and he wouldn't let go until he was sure the egg was safe. Of course, it probably wasn't, considering they were flying over the city, but as long as Blake didn't let go, things would be okay.

Probably.

Blake was aware that things would change as soon as they landed, though. Right now, the dragon had grabbed him because he'd been holding the egg. As soon as he could, he would probably drop down and eat Blake, then take the egg and leave. Blake wasn't looking forward to it, and he hated that he'd put himself into this situation. Still, he wouldn't change it. The egg had been in danger, and he'd saved it. Even if this dragon wasn't the father of the egg, the egg was probably safer in his hands than with Blake's boss.

Blake had to think. The problem was that it was hard to do while he was flying, with the wind whipping against his skin, hurting him and messing up his hair. It was strange not to feel anything under his feet while in a standing position. Then of course, there was the puking thing. Blake's stomach was churning, and he wondered what the dragon would think if he puked all over his paw.

He had to do something, though. The dragon had talked to him instead of killing him right away, so that gave him hope. He'd already told the dragon that he'd only been trying to help. Maybe he would have the time to make the dragon listen to him, and hopefully, the dragon would believe he didn't have anything to do with the theft.

Blake's boss should have known things wouldn't be easy. How could they be? No one was crazy enough to steal a dragon egg, or at least, Blake had thought so. He'd obviously been wrong. His boss *had* been stupid enough, and now, Blake was going to pay the price for that.

Sheldon was right. Blake's curiosity would kill him, and sooner rather than later, apparently.

Blake huffed. Sheldon wouldn't understand why he'd taken the egg, or why he hadn't given it to the dragon right away. That was okay. Blake and Sheldon were different, and Blake didn't expect him to understand. But Sheldon *had* been right. It might get Blake killed, and he wasn't looking forward to it. He hoped the dragon would give him time to text his brother to tell him he wasn't coming back. Sheldon would be hurt, but at least he'd know. Having Blake disappear from one day to the next without knowing what had happened to him would be worse than knowing he was dead.

So Blake waited. There was nothing else he could do. He hoped the dragon would believe him when he explained, but then, humans had stolen the egg. They'd been horrible to dragons since the beginning of time. They'd killed them and tortured them up to the point that there were very few dragons left, or at least, that was what everyone thought. But Blake had just seen five dragons tonight, so maybe, there were more of them left than was known.

Either way, he probably would never find out. Even if the dragon didn't kill him, he would no doubt abandon him wherever they landed, and Blake would have to find his way back home. Even if he managed that, his boss would be there, and he would no doubt kill Blake for what he'd done.

It was a lose-lose situation, and Blake was right in the middle of it. He had no idea what would happen, but he prayed that by the end of the evening, he would still be alive — and in one piece.

What's going on? Orran asked his team. He needed to know. He had to make sure they were okay.

I'm fine, Morven answered.

Orran relaxed, but this wasn't over yet. *What about the others?*

I'm with Octavia and Hogan.

What about Slavin?

I don't know.

I'm here, Slavin said.

Orran finally allowed himself to relax completely. They were safe, all of them. *Is everyone okay?*

A few cuts here and there, but I'll be fine, Slavin answered. *What about you? Do you have the egg?*

Orran briefly looked down. He could see the human clutching at his claws and the egg, which was both a relief and an annoyance. He had no idea what he would do with the man. He supposed he would find out soon enough, though. *I have the egg,* he confirmed.

Good, Morven said. *Humans are still following us, though.*

Orran didn't like the sound of that. *Can you lose them somewhere?* He wouldn't have a problem with Morven killing the humans if it became necessary, but he didn't want Morven to draw attention to himself and the others. Humans had been hunting dragons for decades. They deserved a bit of pain, especially after stealing a baby dragon. The egg was still intact, but there was still a baby inside, and they were without their mother. Besides, Orran could too easily imagine what those humans were planning to do with the egg. They deserved to pay for what they'd done and what they'd been planning to do, as far as he was concerned. They also deserved to pay for trying to kill Orran and the others when they'd tried to retrieve the egg.

We'll try to leave them behind, but we can't make any promises, Hogan said.

It's safer if you stay away, though, Morven added. *We'll contact you again as soon as we can. Slavin, if you're not being followed, you should head back to the palace. Tell them we're fine and that we're still dealing with humans. We can't go back now, not without leading them there, and that's the last thing we want, even though some of them have already been inside the palace.*

Orran agreed. He didn't like it, though. He wasn't looking forward to spending any length of time with the human he was holding, but apparently, it was going to be a *thing*.

He didn't know what to think of the human. He didn't even know if he believed that he'd been trying to help. Could that be the truth? It *was* true that the human hadn't been hurting the egg. Now that Orran thought about the situation he'd flown in on, he realized the man had been trying to keep the egg away from the other humans. That might mean he wasn't lying when he said that, but how could Orran be sure? There was no way. He couldn't read minds, and he didn't know this guy. He couldn't trust him. That still left him the problem of what to do with him.

We'll get the humans to chase us away from you, Morven said.

Orran didn't like *that* idea, either. *Are you sure? You could get hurt. You saw that gun they had.* Orran had never seen anything like it, and he wasn't looking forward to seeing it again. It seemed like the humans had been working on finding a way to shoot down dragons, and they might have succeeded.

We'll do our best not to get shot, but if you have the egg, you are the one who needs to be protected. Don't worry about us.

Orran snorted. *Don't worry about you? Really?*

I know it won't be easy. Trust me. I'm worried about you right now, and my first instinct is to join you wherever you are. But we both know better. If we want the egg to be safe, we need to do this the right way. Don't worry about the humans, not until you see them. We'll make sure they follow us instead of you.

Not worrying about the humans was going to be impossible since he was holding one, but Orran agreed. *All right. But let me know what's happening. I want a report every few hours if possible.*

I'll see what I can do, and the same goes for everyone else. Stay safe, Orran. I want to see you in one piece when we get back to the palace.

That ended the conversation. Orran turned his attention back to where he was going and to the human he was holding. He'd studied humans and their world, just like every other dragon, so he knew more or less where he was. He could probably find his way to a safe place, at least for a bit, but what was he going to do with the human? If he took him with him, then the human would see where he was. That meant he could attack or call his friends.

But maybe not. If the human hadn't been lying, those other humans didn't have anything to do with him. He wouldn't call them to get the egg because he'd been trying to protect the egg.

Orran had no idea what to do.

It should be easy for him to deal with one tiny human. He could kill the human, or even abandon him somewhere isolated. As long as Orran made sure he didn't have a phone, he wouldn't be able to call for help, and he'd have to find his way back to the city. It would take him a while, and Orran would be back at the palace by the time it happened. But for some reason, Orran wasn't looking forward to doing that. If the human was really attempting to protect the egg, Orran couldn't treat him like that.

He shook his head, and the movement made his entire body move. The human shrieked, and laughter rumbled in Orran's chest. No matter what happened, the next few moments were going to be fun.

He looked around. He was flying over a forest, and he couldn't see anyone following them. It was probably safe to land right now, at least to check in on the egg. Besides, he and the human needed to talk. If something happened, Orran could leave the human, take the egg, and fly away.

He lowered until he found a nice sized clearing. It was hidden, since it was in the middle of the trees, so it would make it hard for the humans to find him if they were following. He had to let go of the human he was holding before landing, and the human took the opportunity to try to run away as soon as his feet touched the ground.

Orran rolled his eyes, then grabbed him again. He gave him a good shake, and the human squeaked. At least, he'd stopped moving. Orran sat down and brought the human close to his face. He peered at the human's face, wondering how to communicate that he wanted the man to stay still. They were eye to eye, or at least, to one of Orran's eyes. His face was as big as half the human, and it was obvious the human was very much aware of that. Orran stared him in the eyes until the human finally nodded and said, "Fine. I'll stay still. I got the message."

Orran nodded once, then let go. He paused, expecting the human to betray him and try to run away again, but to his surprise, he stayed right where he was. Orran waited one moment longer, then shifted.

The human gasped. Orran had no idea why, and he didn't care. The human was still holding the egg, and when Orran reached out, the human clutched the egg to his chest.

"I can't give it to you," the human said.

Orran growled. "It belongs to me more than it belongs to you."

"I'm aware of that. Don't think I'm not. But I need to be sure the egg will be in good hands. I would never forgive myself if I gave it to the wrong person and it got hurt."

That wasn't what Orran had expected. He wanted to explain what had happened so the human would see he could be trusted, but he couldn't. Humans couldn't know about the queen or the palace where Orran lived. The queen had worked hard to make the palace invisible through magic and to make sure humans didn't remember it was there. Orran couldn't ruin everything just to give an explanation to this man.

So he reached for the egg again. He was fast, much faster than the human, but he wasn't surprised when the human clung to the egg. Orran pulled again, and the egg finally slipped. The human would have none of that, though, and he tried to tighten his hold on the egg. He also kicked out, and his foot hit Orran's thigh. Orran cried out, not having expected it, and he watched in horror as the egg tumbled to the ground.

The egg had cracked. Blake had heard the sound as if it resonated through his brain, and he quickly fell to his knee, reaching for the egg and cradling it. He checked it over, needing to make sure it was okay, but the crack was evident. He didn't know what it meant for the baby dragon inside, and he wasn't sure he should ask. The dragon shifter—because that was what the man standing in front of him had to be—would probably tear his head off at the first peep. Hell, he would probably tear Blake's head off just for taking the egg, even though Blake had been trying to help.

And what a help he'd been. It looked like he'd killed the baby dragon, and he didn't know how he would be able to live with himself if that was what had happened.

To his surprise, the egg rattled, then the crack became larger. He looked at the adult dragon, knowing the horror had to show on his face, but to his surprise, the man just crouched next to them and poked his finger at the crack.

Blake pulled the egg away, holding it closer to his chest. "What are you doing?" he asked.

The dragon cocked his head. He was gorgeous, albeit in a strange kind of way. He looked nothing like a human, now that Blake had the time to look at him, but even so, Blake couldn't deny how beautiful he was. His long, flowing blue hair cascaded down his back and shoulders. His eyes were blue, but instead of being round, the pupil was slit, like a snake's — or a dragon's. Most of his skin was the same pale color as Blake's, except for the spots covered in blue scales. Blake had to work hard not to look directly at the dragon's groin, mostly because he'd never seen anything like that. He was pretty sure the dragon was a male, or at least, he'd thought so from the voice, but he didn't have a dick. Blake would know — the guy was naked. He also didn't have breasts, and while Blake had studied dragons in school like everyone else, they hadn't gone deep into dragon anatomy. No one knew how dragons were made except for their obvious appearance, and no one knew that dragons could shift into human beings.

Blake was entirely in the dark, and the egg was still moving. He looked down, wondering what was next. "What's going on?" he asked, hoping the dragon would answer.

"They're coming out."

That much was obvious when a piece of the shell fell. Blake noticed a tiny eye behind it, and he reached for the hole, wondering if he was doing the right thing. He gently took another piece of the shell off, dumping it to the ground.

Between him and the baby dragon, they managed to get him or her out of the egg easily. The baby shook themselves, made a weird purring sound, and looked at Blake.

Then the other dragon reached for it.

Blake didn't have a choice. He could still refuse to hand over the baby, but he doubted he would win this fight. Even if the baby didn't belong with this guy, there was nothing Blake could do about it.

"Will they be okay?" he asked. The baby *looked* okay, but what did Blake know?

The adult dragon's hands brushed against the baby, and to both their surprise, the baby whipped around and growled. Blake's eyes widened when the baby scampered up Blake's arm to settle on his shoulder. They opened their mouth and made a wheezing sound, and smoke came out of it, along with a tiny flame.

"Fire? Really?" the adult dragon asked.

The baby growled again. Blake had no idea what was happening, but it seemed that the baby dragon didn't want to leave him. They certainly didn't seem to want to go with the adult dragon.

The adult dragon held his hands out. "Your mother is waiting for you. You were taken from her, and she misses you. You remember her, don't you?"

The baby cocked their head as if considering what the dragon was saying. Blake was considering it, too. Of course, he'd known the egg had been stolen from someone. Dragon eggs didn't appear from out of nowhere. He hadn't thought about the mother, though. He hadn't had the time to. He'd been trying to keep the egg safe—first from his boss and his friends, and then from the dragon standing in front of him. "Are you the father?" he asked

The dragon looked offended. "Of course not."

Blake reached up and stroke the baby's head. They made a purring sound and half-closed their eyes, clearly in bliss. "Why should I give them to you, then?"

The dragon shook his head. "Because I was sent by their mother to get them back. I need to bring them to her."

"I agree on that, but how can I be sure that's what you're going to do? No offense, but they don't seem to like you very much."

The dragon turned his attention to the baby again, dismissing Blake. "Your mother asked me to bring you back. Don't you want to see her?" He wiggled his fingers, and it really shouldn't have been as adorable as it was. This dragon could kill Blake with one movement, and Blake was more than a little aware of that.

But the baby wasn't moving. They were clinging to Blake's shoulder, their claws digging in painfully. Blake had raised a hand, cupping it around the baby's stomach to keep them in place. He didn't know if the baby needed it, but he did. He could too easily imagine the baby tumbling to the ground.

Blake had no idea what was going on. He wanted to trust the adult dragon. He probably wasn't lying when he said he'd been sent by the baby's mother.

He cleared his throat. "Okay. It's obvious that neither of us trusts the other." The dragon snorted, and Blake ignored him. "My name is Blake. I worked for one of the guys who got the egg. Well, he wasn't there when the egg was stolen, I don't think. But I've always known he was involved in some weird stuff, but I needed the job, so I stayed out of it. Then tonight, a group of guys came in. They all went to his office, then came out and got drunk. I was sent to the office, saw the egg, and knew it wouldn't end well for it if I didn't take it. So I did."

The dragon cocked his head. "Why did you care? It's a dragon. Not a human."

"So? Would anyone allow people to hurt the baby? Because I wouldn't, and neither would my brother." Maybe. Sheldon wasn't a bad guy, but he also wasn't stupid, and he would probably protect himself before he protected the egg.

"You just said you would lose your job over this."

Blake rolled his eyes. "I already did, didn't I? I doubt that if I go back to the city, my boss will welcome me with open arms. Hell, it's more probable that he'll try to kill me than anything else."

"And you knew that before you took the egg?"

"Yeah."

"Yet you still took it. Why? I don't understand."

"Well, welcome to the club, because I don't understand much of anything right now. I have so many questions that I could probably ask them all and I wouldn't be done by

Christmas."

The dragon cocked his head again, and Blake was starting to realize that he did it when he didn't understand what Blake was talking about. Blake wasn't about to explain, though. Instead, he cleared his throat. "Look, I apologize for what happened. I probably should have handed over the egg. Hell, you could have killed me and just taken it. Instead, you saved the egg and me in the process. So thank you. I know what would have happened to me if you hadn't taken me with you, and I'm grateful for that. I also apologize for not trusting you, but I hope you can see why I didn't. I'm still not sure if I can trust you, to be honest, and it's obvious the baby isn't going anywhere without me."

The dragon growled. "What are you saying?"

Blake had no idea what he was saying. "I'm not sure. Well, I don't think the baby wants to leave me, and I need you to make sure they're okay. Can you check, please?"

The dragon blinked. "You worry about the baby."

"Of course I worry. Didn't you hear what I said? Can you please check him or her?" Blake prayed that nothing had happened to the baby. He'd been trying to save it, but maybe he'd made things worse. He had no idea how he would deal with that or how he would fix things, but he supposed he was about to find out.

Orran didn't understand why the human seemed to be so worried about the baby, but he was grateful for it. The baby had ended up in the hands of someone who cared, instead of someone who would hurt them. "They appear to be healthy, yes."

The human — Blake. He'd told Orran his name — sighed in relief. "Thank God. I don't know what I would have done if I'd hurt him. Or her?"

Blake couldn't tell from the distance, and he wasn't about to say that. "The egg was about to crack when it was stolen, so you don't have to be worried. It was its time. That was why it was laid and ended up stolen in the first place."

Blake blinked. "You're not going to explain any of that even if I ask, are you?"

Orran grinned at him. "You're right. I'm not. And I need to take the baby back to their mother."

Blake shrugged. "I doubt I'll be able to stop you if you try to take the baby. Not for long, anyway. You're welcome to try."

Orran narrowed his eyes at him. It was obvious he'd realized that for some reason, the baby had decided to cling to him. Orran had no idea why that was. Even when they'd been in the egg, the baby had been aware of what was happening around them, as much as a baby could. Blake wasn't even a dragon. The fact that the baby didn't want to come didn't make sense.

Still, Orran had to try, at the very least.

"Come on," he tried to coax. "I'm sure you want to see your mother."

The baby mirrored Blake's expression, narrowing their eyes at him. Then they huffed, and a tiny flame came out of their mouth.

Blake jumped, but thankfully, he was holding the baby with one hand, so they didn't tumble to the ground. Orran was amused, both at the human's reaction and at the way the baby treated him. Baby dragons knew who their carrying parent was. They spent a long time inside their parent's body while the egg was being formed and while the baby incubated. The baby knew Blake wasn't their father, yet for whatever reason, they had latched onto him, and Orran was starting to realize that he would have a hard time taking them away.

He had no idea what to do. The baby was trying to protect Blake, thinking that Orran was a danger to him. And Orran would have been if he'd been intent on hurting Blake. He wasn't, though. He had no intention of hurting the human, especially after everything that had happened. He wasn't sure he could trust Blake, but he believed what Blake had said. It fit with everything he knew and everything he'd seen.

"It doesn't look like they want to go."

Orran glared at Blake. "I can see that."

Blake bit his lower lip. For a human, he was kind of beautiful. Not beautiful like Orran was used to, but he couldn't deny there was an alien beauty to the man.

He rubbed his face with his hands. He had to do something, but he didn't know what. He didn't usually deal with babies. He didn't have any children himself, not yet, and he wasn't a babysitter. It was the first time in forever that he had to deal with a little one, and he didn't know how to convince the baby to come to him. Maybe he could wait until the baby fell asleep. That way, he would be able to take them away from Blake without a problem. That meant spending more time with Blake than Orran was comfortable spending with a human, though. "I'm Orran," he said.

Blake blinked. "Oh, look at that. You have a name."

Orran glared at him. "I have a name, yes, and I just told it to you."

"Does that mean you're finally agreeing that the baby isn't going anywhere without me?"

Orran hesitated. He didn't want to agree with whatever the human was saying, but he couldn't deny the guy was right. "I don't want to force them away from you," he finally explained. "For whatever reason, they think you're safe."

Blake looked offended. "That's because I am. I told you. I was only trying to help."

And maybe he had been. But Orran had no way of

knowing what would have happened if Blake hadn't taken the egg from his boss's office. He also didn't care. He wasn't about to start thinking about what-ifs.

But he couldn't take Blake home. That just couldn't be done. The palace was home only to dragons, and there was a good reason for that. Humans had been hurting dragons for hundreds of years. That was why dragons had fled the cities and isolated themselves. That was why the palace was hidden, just like every other dragon home.

But Orran couldn't explain any of that to Blake. He would be giving away too many secrets, and that wasn't something he could do, no matter how many questions Blake had.

Blake sighed and gently rubbed the baby's side. "Look," he said.

That was something he often said, and Orran shouldn't find it endearing. It wasn't.

"You don't trust me, and I don't trust you," Blake continued. "I doubt that will change anytime soon. But for whatever reason, your baby wants to stay with me. I know that you don't want me to stick around, and that's fine. I get it. I'm human, and you're both dragons. We have no reason to trust each other. But it's also obvious you're not going to take the baby by force."

Orran shook his head. "Of course not." And not only because the queen would have his head if he did something like that. The first hours after a baby dragon was born were important. It was when they found out who their family was, and when they started learning the world. For whatever reason, the baby had decided that Blake was an acceptable friend, and Orran didn't have an explanation for that. He didn't need one, either. It was what it was. He had no doubt that if he took the baby away, the baby would cry and be angry at him. He was ready to face that—he was ready to face the queen. She would understand when he explained.

But the baby wouldn't even let him step close to Blake, and that was a problem. "You're right. I don't trust you," Orran admitted.

Blake smiled sadly. "That's what I was talking about, yes. You still want to take the baby, and I get it. I have no right to it. I also don't know if I can trust you, but again, you could take them away from me without too many problems if you didn't care about hurting them. Instead, you haven't, which makes me realize that you *do* care for them. You're probably not lying when you say that you've been sent by their mother. But they're not going to go with you just like that. You're going to have to find a way around that, which means you'll have to spend some time with me."

Blake was right, no matter how little Orran liked it. He couldn't take Blake with them when they headed back to the palace, but it did look like he was going to have to spend the next few hours with a human.

He didn't know whether to be afraid of that or relish the opportunity.

Orran was torn. That much was obvious even to Blake, who didn't have a good sense of observation. He understood that. Blake was torn, too. On the one hand, he knew Orran could kill him and take the baby without a thought, but on the other, Orran seemed to care for the baby.

For whatever reason, Blake did, too. He was touched that the baby had clung to him. He hadn't expected anything like this when he'd rescued the egg, but he still didn't regret it. Even if Orran decided to kill him eventually, he wouldn't regret it. He'd done the right thing. He'd saved the baby from his boss and the man's horrible friends, and he would do it again if he had to.

Blake allowed himself to relax. As long as the baby was on

him, Orran wouldn't hurt him. He was sure of that. "The baby won't let go of me," he said. "I also can't go back. I'll be killed as soon as I step foot in the city. I saved the egg. If my boss is still alive, he's going to be pissed, and he's going to take it out on me." Of course, Orran probably didn't care about that, but Blake did. He would rather keep all his limbs attached to his body, thank you very much.

"What are you suggesting?" Orran asked.

Blake wasn't sure, but he had to say something. "You have to take the baby back to their mother. That's what you said."

Orran nodded once. "I do. That is why the other dragons and I were there in the first place. To get the egg back."

Except now, they didn't have an egg anymore. They had a baby dragon who had made himself at home on Blake's shoulder. "I could come with you," Blake said.

"To the mother?"

"Yes. I mean, the baby doesn't want to let go of me. I can't go back. I'm not saying I have to move in with you or anything, but I'd rather not have to head to the city. I never wanted to hurt the baby. I just want to help him or her. I promise."

"I could just wait until the baby is asleep and take them."

Blake was aware of that. "You could. What will you do when they wake up, though? When they realize I'm not with you and freak out? Also, how will you take them away? In your dragon form? How does that work? They can't exactly hold on to your back while you fly, but I can say from experience that your claws aren't that comfortable."

Orran's eyes narrowed. "What are you suggesting?" he asked again.

Blake had no idea. Still, he pressed on. It was his one chance to make it out of the situation okay. "I'll come with you. I'll carry the baby, since they seem to be attached to me. I'd promise you I won't hurt them, but I already did, and saying it once more won't change what you think about me. But let's face reality. You're a dragon. You could crush me with one hand, burn me to a crisp, and stomp me to death without breaking a sweat." Not in this form, but in his dragon form, he definitely could. Blake was trying very hard to focus on the most important thing in this situation, though, so he made sure to look at Orran's face rather than at his unusual body. "So I'm going to come with you when you take the baby back to his mother. I don't know how far away you have to fly, but it doesn't matter to me."

"Don't you have a family to go back to? They can protect you," Orran said.

The thought of his family made Blake's chest feel tight. "I only have my brother, and we're not that close." They'd been working on that, but they were so different, and Blake knew he was lucky Sheldon even wanted to talk to him.

"You have nothing to go back to? That's what you're saying?"

"I say it because it's true." Blake only had a tiny apartment, a few sets of clothes, and nothing more. He had Sheldon, but Sheldon had his own life. He had a good job, and he was still in contact with the family. He might miss Blake in the beginning, but that wouldn't last long. Blake was convinced of that. He cleared his throat. "I'm not telling you I'm planning to stay. I realize it's probably not possible." Even though he had never done anything to hurt dragons, he could understand that dragons wouldn't trust him. Hell, he'd found out one of their secrets already, that dragons weren't animals like everyone else thought. They could become humans, and they could talk. It was obvious that Orran was intelligent, probably even more than Blake. It was like talking with another human being, and Blake would never be able to forget that. He didn't want to. If he made it out of the situation alive, he would cherish the memories. He would also keep them to himself, though. He owed that to Orran.

Orran had only been trying to rescue the egg, but he'd risked a lot. Blake supposed Orran was lucky that Blake was the one who'd found out his secret, and that no one else had seen him. It could have gone so much worse.

Orran's shoulders slumped, and Blake held his breath. There was nothing else he could say or do to convince Orran that this was the best thing to do. "All right," Orran eventually said.

Blake didn't allow himself to hope, not yet. "What are you agreeing to?"

"You can come with me, at least for now. The baby needs to be close to you. That much is obvious. I don't want to tear them away from you, since they consider you friendly. But it won't last forever, and you can't meet the mother. It's forbidden."

That was much more than what Blake had expected to begin with, and he was relieved. "We can talk about all of this later."

Orran's eyes narrowed. "This is already a big concession. Don't think you'll be able to wiggle your way into more of them."

Blake didn't, but if there was something to be said about him, it was that he always had hope. He had to. There wouldn't be a reason for him to live if he didn't believe, if he didn't *hope*, that he could have a better life.

Maybe this was his ticket to that better life. He didn't know, but he would find out soon enough.

CHAPTER THREE

Blake was freezing. He'd slept curled around the baby, and their presence had helped, but it hadn't worked miracles. Blake's back felt like it was made of ice, and he wasn't sure he could uncurl himself and get to his feet, even though it was morning and he needed to do just that.

He doubted Orran would want to hang around. He'd been surprised when Orran had suggested they stay where they'd landed for the night, but he supposed the dragon had made that exception because of the baby. They'd just been born, and they were no doubt confused about the world. Maybe they were confused about Blake, too. Maybe that was why they'd latched onto him.

Not that Blake had a problem with that. If anything, he was grateful. He was pretty sure Orran would have sent him back to the city, and that wouldn't have been good for him. Instead, it looked like he was going to travel with two dragons for a while, and he was excited. It was better than going back home and getting killed, that was for sure. There was also the fact that he'd always been fascinated with dragons, and now he had the chance to be close to two of them. And of course, he'd found out that dragons were actually shifters.

Some people would pay gold to get their hands on that information, but Blake wasn't planning on telling anyone. If he was honest with himself, he was still hoping that he'd have a chance to stay with the baby once they got to the baby's mother. Orran had been clear — Blake wouldn't be allowed to do that, because they couldn't take the risk that he'd lead other humans to wherever they lived. Blake understood that, but he didn't like it, and he was kind of hoping that Orran would get to know him and would realize that he truly wasn't a danger.

The baby sneezed, and a small flame shot from his mouth. Blake just had the time to scramble away, and he fell on his ass, laughing. The baby blinked at him, then grinned, exposing their teeth. Blake opened his arms, and the baby scrambled into them. Blake closed his arms around them, then kissed the top of their head.

When he looked up, Orran was awake, standing close by and staring at him and the baby. Blake looked away, his cheeks heating. He realized it had to be weird for Orran. Humans usually killed dragons, yet here Blake was, cuddling one. He didn't care what Orran thought about him or the way he behaved, though. He just hoped that Orran would realize he wasn't planning on hurting anyone, least of all the baby. They were precious, and they deserved to be protected.

"Good morning," Blake said as he got to his feet. It wasn't easy to do with the baby clinging to his chest, but he managed.

Orran seemed to shake himself. "You snore," he said

Blake spluttered. "I'm sorry?"

"I said, you snore."

"I heard that. I just wasn't sure I'd heard it right, though. It's rude."

"It's the truth. That's not being rude. That's being honest."

Blake rolled his eyes. He knew he wasn't going to win. "You got a fire going," he said, shuffling closer.

"You have an astounding power of observation," Orran said, his voice dry.

Blake had no idea what to think about the dragon's behavior. He knew they weren't friends. Orran had been quite clear about that, and Blake hadn't expected him to change his mind and suddenly decide he could trust him during the night. He supposed it was better than the open hostility Orran had had toward him yesterday. At least Orran wasn't trying to kill him, and Blake counted that as a win.

"You could have lit that fire during the night," he whined as he moved even closer. "I was cold."

"And I should care, why? The baby wasn't cold. That's all that mattered."

Blake kind of agreed. Still. "There you go, being rude again. Has no one taught you how to be nice?"

"I'm not nice. Nice gets you killed."

Blake winced. He supposed that from Orran's point of view, that was the truth. He was a dragon, after all. They were big, they spat fire, and they could stomp any human to death, but they were still killed by them. It couldn't be easy to deal with, just like having to deal with Blake couldn't be easy. But Blake wasn't going anywhere, so Orran needed to get used to his presence.

"There's food. I hunted." Orran tilted his chin toward the fire, and Blake noticed the meat there. It was already cooked, and his stomach grumbled. Still, he had things to do before he could eat.

He turned his attention to the baby. "Good morning," he said, scratching the bottom of their chin. "I propose that we get you cleaned up, then we can eat. What do you think about that?"

The baby gurgled, and Blake decided it was a yes. He didn't have much to clean the baby with, so he used the bottom of his t-shirt, raising it and gently stroking the baby's face with it. The baby wasn't that dirty, but Blake always felt better in the morning when he washed his face or at least tried to groom himself. Maybe the same would go for the baby.

Once that was done, Blake crouched next to the fire. He took a piece of meat—he couldn't identify it, and he wasn't about to ask—and held it out to the baby. He wasn't surprised when the baby gently took the piece of meat from his fingers. He grinned. He had no idea how to deal with babies, human or dragon, but he was relieved to see the baby was eating.

He continued feeding them, smiling with every bite they took. Then, he realized he should probably have asked before feeding a baby dragon he didn't know anything about. He looked at Orran, and Orran was once again staring. "They can eat meat, right?"

Orran blinked. "Of course. What else should they be eating?"

"I don't know. Human babies get milk. They can't eat meat until they're around one year old, I think." Although Blake could be wrong—it had been a while since he'd seen his nephews and nieces.

He cleared his throat. He didn't want to think about his family. He never wanted to think about them. He finished feeding the baby, then cleaned their face once again with his t-shirt. He was ruining the thing, but he didn't care.

"Why did you do that?" Orran asked.

Blake frowned and looked at him as he pushed a piece of meat into his mouth. "What?" he asked.

Orran wrinkled his nose, probably in disgust. "You fed the baby first. You didn't eat until now that you're sure they're sated. You cleaned them, too, using your clothes. Why did you do that?"

Blake frowned. "Why are you so surprised? They're a baby. It's obvious they come first."

"They're a dragon."

"So are you, so what? You should know it doesn't change anything to me." Orran hesitated, then nodded. Blake didn't want to talk about this, so instead, he asked, "What now?"

Orran's expression hardened. "We're going to fly home."

"And you won't tell me where home is, right?"

"I don't trust you, human. I don't know you. The only

reason you're allowed to come with me is that the baby won't let go of you."

It wasn't a threat, but Blake could read between the lines. If the baby decided to leave Blake's arms, if they decided they didn't like Blake anymore, Blake would be left behind.

He tightened his arms around the baby, then forced himself to smile at Orran. "That's okay for now. We can talk about it again later."

Orran looked like he wanted to throttle Blake, but that wasn't new, either. There was always someone angry with Blake.

While Blake finished eating and took care of the baby again, Orran cleaned their encampment. There wasn't much to do, and soon enough, he was shifting.

It was impressive, almost as much as Orran's human form. It was alien in a different way, and while Blake couldn't wait to see Orran's human form again, he also loved this one.

It was also much more intimidating, though.

Orran stared at Blake. Blake stared back, not sure what to do. Was Orran going to grab him with his claws again? Because there was no way that he was silently telling Blake to climb onto his back, right?

Orran was still staring, and Blake had no idea what to do, so he didn't do anything.

Orran didn't understand humans. He wasn't surprised he didn't, although he couldn't help but wonder if maybe Blake was a special case. He continued staring at Blake, wondering what was going on and why the human wasn't climbing onto his back. He *continued* staring until Blake cleared his throat, then said, "I'm not sure what you want me to do."

Orran had thought it was obvious. Clearly, he'd been wrong. He huffed, then moved his snout closer to Blake, who stumbled back. Since he didn't want to shift again, Orran pointedly looked at Blake, then turned his head so he could look at his own back. When he looked at Blake again, Blake's eyes had gone wide. "You want me to climb on your back?" Blake asked.

Orran nodded. That was *exactly* what he wanted, and he was quite relieved Blake had understood it.

Blake hesitated. "Are you sure?" Orran rolled his eyes. He wouldn't have suggested it if he wasn't sure, would he? Blake still had something to say, though. "I mean, I would have thought it would be disrespectful. You're not an animal. You're a human being, even though you can shift into a dragon. I don't want to hurt you by being disrespectful."

Orran blinked. Once again, the human had done something he wasn't expecting. He had no idea how to deal with the man. He wanted to believe that Blake was like every other human being he'd encountered in his life — mean, ready to do anything to become rich and powerful. Instead, he'd been watching Blake since yesterday. He'd seen how Blake had made sure to protect the baby from the cold, curling himself around them. He'd seen how Blake had taken care of the baby this morning, giving them food and cleaning them as if they were Blake's child. He was nothing like Orran had expected, and he didn't know what to do with that. He supposed the answer was nothing, at least for now.

They were wasting time — precious time they probably didn't have. Once again, he looked at his back, then huffed, smoke coming out of his nose. Blake took a step back, but he didn't look scared. Instead, he looked excited, even though he was still hesitant. "Are you sure?" he repeated.

Orran lowered his head until they were eye to eye. He huffed again, bathing Blake's face with smoke.

Blake coughed and took a step back. "I get it, I get it. You're sure about that. Okay. I'm going to climb on your back, and please, don't try to throw me to the ground."

Orran was amused, much more than he probably should be. He chuckled, the sound coming out rumbling, and lowered his body. Blake needed Orran to help him climb, and while Orran wasn't crazy about that, he also couldn't deny that Blake was making sure the baby was okay and safe before he himself was, and that meant something. It would mean a lot to the queen, too, and Orran would make sure she knew.

Blake finally climbed on top of Orran.

It was odd to feel someone riding him this way. Orran wasn't used to it. All the people he knew were dragons, and they didn't need to be carried around. It sometimes happened when people were wounded, but it hadn't in a while, at least not to Orran.

Once he was sure that Blake was settled, Orran took flight. He opened his wings and pushed with his thighs, rising from the ground. He heard Blake screech, but the shock was gone in seconds, then, the laughter started. Blake whooped as soon as they were in the air. He sounded happy, and Orran had to turn around to look at him.

Blake was beaming, but he gently pushed at Orran's head when he saw Orran was looking. "Watch the sky. I wouldn't want you to crash us." His voice was barely audible over the wind, but Orran found himself smiling. He wasn't going to crash. He knew what he was doing.

Once again, Blake surprised him. He'd thought the human would be terrified of flying, and he had been yesterday. That probably had been more Orran's fault than Blake's, though. Orran hadn't warned him. He'd just grabbed him and flown away, and that would probably have terrified anyone. Now, Blake knew what was going on. He'd been the one to climb onto Orran's back. He was clinging to him with one hand, holding the baby to his chest with the other. They looked kind of adorable, even though Orran would have never admitted that to anyone.

He didn't understand the human. He wasn't surprised about that, because humans thought differently than dragons. That much had always been obvious to him. No, what surprised him was that he *wanted* to understand Blake. It was an alien feeling. He wasn't sure he liked it, but he supposed that didn't matter.

He'd never met a human. He'd killed several, but he didn't count that as meeting them, and Blake was nothing like he'd expected, especially when it came to the baby. He'd thought Blake would be disgusted, or that he would consider the baby an animal, maybe like one of those dogs that humans seem to like so much. Instead, he was treating the baby like he would a human baby. He was taking care of them, feeding them and cleaning them, making sure they were warm enough when they slept.

Maybe he wasn't a bad person after all. Maybe he'd been telling the truth when he'd said that he was just trying to help. Orran was still wary of genuinely believing that, but he couldn't deny what his eyes could see.

He lightly shook his head, then focused on the problem at hand. *Morven?* he called out.

Morven would only answer if he was in his dragon form, and Orran prayed he was. He needed to be. Orran had to find out what had happened to his team.

Orran? Morven finally answered after a few moments.

Orran had never felt so relieved. *You're okay?*

As okay as we can be. Tired, but none of us is injured. What about you? Is the egg okay?

Orran hadn't told Morven the egg had opened. *The* baby *is fine.*

Baby? Does that mean the egg opened?

It did. And for whatever reason, the baby decided they like the human.

There was a pause, then Morven's laugher reached Orran's

mind. *You have a human, too?*

One, yes. I didn't expect to have to carry him with me, but he wouldn't give me the egg.

He wanted to keep it for himself?

Orran wasn't surprised that was where Morven's mind had gone. *Not the way you think. He wasn't sure he could trust me, even though I'm a dragon. He didn't know if the baby belonged to me. From what he said, he stole the egg from his boss, one of the men who attacked us. He wanted to make sure the egg would be okay and that his boss wouldn't hurt it or the baby inside it. Of course, we ruined everything by getting there when we did.* Or maybe they'd helped Blake. He'd been in trouble when they'd arrived.

And you believe him? Morven sounded skeptical, and Orran didn't blame him.

So far, he hasn't done anything that would lead me to think he was lying, so I believe him, yes. Besides, the baby wouldn't allow me to leave him behind. They haven't left Blake's arms since they came out of the egg.

There was a pause, then Morven asked, *Blake?*

Orran berated himself for letting that tidbit of information slip out. *The human. That's his name. Anyway. What happened with the other humans?*

As far as I can see, they're still following us, so that's good for you. You focus on getting the baby home. We'll take care of the humans.

Orran still didn't like this, but he knew he didn't have a choice. His main job was to keep the baby safe, and that was what he would do. *Let me know if I can do anything,* he told Morven.

I will, but the only thing we need is for the baby to get home safe.

And Orran was going to do everything he could to make that happen.

Blake was relieved when they finally landed. He loved flying, to his own surprise, but riding a dragon was uncomfortable, to say the least. He supposed that now he understood why people rode horses with a saddle. His legs felt like they wouldn't be able to move if he tried hopping to the ground, but he had to try.

He slid to the side, almost falling on his face. He just had time to catch himself on Orran's flank, then put his trembling legs down. His feet touched the ground, and he stumbled. He never let go of the baby. He didn't want the baby to get hurt, and he clutched them to his chest, smiling when they cooed in what sounded like encouragement.

Orran shifted. Blake could tell something was wrong as soon as he saw Orran's face, but he wasn't sure it was his place to ask what was going on. Probably not. He doubted Orran would explain even if he *did* ask, anyway. Instead of asking the questions that he was burning to ask, Blake turned his attention to the baby. He scratched under the baby's chin, smiling when smoke came out of the baby's nose.

"I contacted my team," Orran suddenly said.

Blake blinked. "What do you mean?"

"The other dragons, the ones who were with me when I grabbed you."

"I realized that was who you were talking about. I'm just not sure I understand what you mean by contacting them. You didn't use a phone. Hell, you were in your dragon form, and you were flying."

Orran hesitated.

Blake knew he would only explain if he wanted to, so he turned his attention back to the baby. He sat on the ground, crossing his legs, and the baby settled in between them, looking up at him. Blake ran his fingertips down the baby's back, marveling at the smoothness of the scales. For some reason, he'd always imagined dragons to be cold to the touch. He wasn't sure why. Maybe because snakes were cold. Right? Blake had no idea. He'd never touched a snake, either. Hell, he'd never seen a real snake.

But the baby was warm, and their scales were soft. It was surprising, and Blake couldn't help but wonder what other misconceptions he had about dragons.

"When we're in our dragon form, we can communicate with our minds," Orran said.

Blake frowned. He supposed that answered a lot of questions he had. Still, he had many others. He wasn't sure what to think about the fact that most of those questions had to do with Orran's human body.

He hadn't missed the fact that when Orran shifted to his human form, he was entirely naked. He'd been trying very hard not to stare, but sometimes, it was complicated. It was easier to focus on the questions, but he wasn't sure Orran would answer them. Hell, *he* probably wouldn't if someone asked him about that.

"What did they say?" he asked instead.

"That the humans were following them. They seem to think the egg is with them, and that's a good thing for us."

Blake slowly nodded. "It's good because it keeps those guys away from the egg, or rather, the baby, but it puts your friends at risk."

Orran seemed surprised that Blake could understand that. "It does, yes."

Maybe he needed to be distracted. "Can I ask you some questions about dragons?"

"I can't promise I'll answer them," Orran warned. He looked wary again, and Blake hated it.

He understood why Orran didn't trust him. Hell, he didn't think he fully trusted Orran, either. It was still hurtful, though. "I never knew dragons had a human form," he began.

"That's because we never wanted you to find out."

"I understand." And he truly did. Why would dragons want humans to know that they could become human, too? It would give them another way to hurt dragons, and that was the last thing they needed. "I get why you don't want to answer all my questions, and that's fine. I was just wondering about your human form. I mean, it's obvious you're not *entirely* human."

Orran arched a brow. "It is?"

Blake rolled his eyes. "For one, I'm pretty sure your blue hair is natural. Humans don't have blue hair." Even the ones who did didn't have hair as gorgeous as Orran's. It was an incredible kind of blue, a blue Blake couldn't describe. He would have to be a poet to do it, or maybe a songwriter. It flowed down Orran's neck, covering his naked shoulders, looking like a silky cloud, or maybe a wave.

Parts of Orran's body were human. He had two arms and legs, and obviously, a head. He didn't have a tail when he was human, which was a relief. His skin was pale like Blake's, at least in some places. In others, it was blue and appeared scaly, just like his dragon skin. He was also hairless, except for his head, which was . . . interesting.

Then there was the problem of Orran's groin. Blake had never seen anything like that, and he hated himself even for looking at it. He didn't think of Orran as a sexual being because he had no idea how that worked for dragons. His nosiness had already put him in trouble more than enough in recent days, though, so he didn't ask why Orran didn't have a dick but rather what looked like a pouch. It wasn't his business.

He shrugged. "I'm just saying that you're kind of different."

"I wouldn't know about that, would I? I've never seen a human body, not naked."

Blake blinked. "Never?"

"I seldom leave the pa — the place where I live," Orran said. "None of us do. The only reason we leave is to defend it, and we never go far. So no. I've never seen a naked human body. I don't know what you look like under your clothes."

Blake's cheeks felt heated, and he looked away. He kind of wanted to offer his own body for perusal, but he knew better than to do that, too. He looked down at the baby and smiled when he saw they'd fallen asleep. "What about the baby? Is it a boy or a girl? I've been using *them* to talk about them, but I'd like to know." And he wished he could give them a better name than *the baby*.

Orran moved closer. "It's a boy."

Blake frowned. "How do you know?"

"I asked him."

It took a second for Blake to understand. "Because you can communicate with dragons when you're in your dragon form."

"Exactly. Dragons don't care if babies are girls or boys. We don't usually ask babies that, but I thought you would want to know. I know humans care about that."

Blake didn't care much, either. What did it matter if the baby was a boy or girl? "Did his mother have a name for him?"

Orran shook his head. "I don't know. She never told me."

"And you're not the father so you can't make that decision."

Orran jerked back. "I already told you I'm not the father."

Blake wasn't sure why that seemed to be so important for him. He supposed it didn't matter. "I don't want to give him a name when his mother would probably give him another one, but I also don't want to keep thinking about him as *the baby*. How about I call him Blue?" Because the baby *was* blue. That was one of the reasons Blake had thought Orran might be the father. Orran was darker, but Blake wondered if maybe once he got older, the baby would become dark, too.

Orran looked surprised. "You want to give him a name?"

"It will be easier to care for him. Of course, I won't if I'm not allowed."

"I don't think his mother would have a problem with it. She'll be grateful that you're taking care of him."

Blake nodded. "Blue it is, then." He wasn't sure why, but it felt like he was taking a step closer to becoming Orran's friend, or at least, to not being his enemy.

Orran was surprised at how curious and respectful Blake was. It was obvious that Blake wasn't used to thinking without putting a gender on the people he met, and Orran supposed that was okay. Gender wasn't as important for dragons, since both males and females laid eggs, but things were different for humans. Still, even though Blake was curious and had asked direct questions, he'd done so in a respectful way, and he'd made sure to tell Orran that it didn't matter to him. That was the main reason Orran hadn't minded telling him.

The baby's mind, just like every young dragon's mind, had been a mess when Orran had contacted him during the flight. He'd wanted to check in on him without having Blake in the middle of things, and the best way and moment to do that was while they were flying and Blake was distracted. Even though gender didn't matter for dragons, the baby had a strong sense of male. Of course, the baby didn't understand what it meant. He didn't have to. It wouldn't change any-thing.

Blue. That was what Blake wanted to call the baby, at least until the queen could give him a proper name. It wasn't as bad as it could have been, Orran supposed. He also under-stood why Blake didn't want to continue calling the baby *baby*.

"Will he ever shift into a human?" Blake asked.

"Eventually, yes. All dragons have the ability to shift. We spend most of our time in our dragon form, though. It's what we're used to. Since we can communicate in our minds, we don't have a reason to take human form." Even though the young dragons seemed to enjoy being human.

Blake wrinkled his nose. "I guess I can see that. I mean, why would you want to look like the people who hurt you so badly?"

Orran probably should stop being surprised at Blake's insight. He might be human, but he understood well how much humans had hurt dragons—and still did. He'd never had anything to do with it, Orran didn't think. But like everyone, he'd heard about the fights, the dragons who had fallen. Now that he knew dragons were human, he probably had a better understanding of how horrible those fights had been and how horrible the trafficking of dragon skin, skulls, bones, and everything else was.

Orran didn't want him to panic, though. Even though he wasn't sure he could trust him, he was sure of one thing—Blake had never hurt a dragon. He wouldn't be taking care of Blue the way he was if he had. It wasn't a caring that meant he was eager to sell Blue. It was in all his movements, in the way he looked at Blue. He truly cared for the baby, even though Orran didn't understand why or how it was possible.

"So you don't shift when you're so small?" Blake asked.

"That's correct. Dragons are always born in their dragon form. They don't usually shift for the first year or so of their life, although that widely differs from dragon to dragon. Some shift much sooner, some don't."

"But he's not going to shift into a fully grown man, right?"

Orran laughed. "Of course not. When he shifts, he will shift into a baby, or a toddler, depending on how old he is when he does." Blake was amusing, if anything.

Blake nodded and looked down at the baby again. "Do you know why he imprinted on me the way he did? I mean, that can't be normal, right?"

Orran didn't know how to answer that. "I think the reason it doesn't usually happen is that dragons don't live with humans. When the egg opens, the parents are there with the baby. That means that the baby usually clings to one of them."

"Why didn't he cling to you, though? He's a dragon, and so are you. I'm just a human. It's not like I took care of the egg before he came out of it."

"But you did. Dragons can hear what happens outside the egg. They might not understand most of it, but they recognize voices, which is how they recognize their parents."

"I talked to the egg," Blake said, stunning Orran. "When I found it, I mean. I talked to it as if it were a baby dragon. I guess it was, in a way. You think that's why he clings to me?"

"I don't know. It's possible. It's also possible that he feels protected with you, and that's one of the most important things for babies."

"The same goes for human babies."

Orran was both amused and amazed by the questions Blake was asking, and by how he behaved. Still, he was worried. He didn't know if he could trust Blake, even though he was starting to think he could. More importantly, he and Blake were in this alone. They wouldn't get any kind of help until they got to the palace, and Orran wasn't sure what to do with that.

They had to protect the baby. That was their main goal, and so far, they'd been doing a good job, especially Blake. Orran didn't resent him. Orran didn't know how to deal with babies, dragon or human or otherwise. He was grateful he didn't have to do it, and that Blake was.

But sooner or later, that would change. He would have to take the baby away from Blake, and he could already tell that the baby wouldn't be happy about it. Orran would also have to contact the palace and make sure that Slavin had arrived. He wanted to tell the queen himself that he'd found her egg and that the baby had been born. He hoped she wouldn't be angry at the fact that her son was clinging to a human, even though it was a human who'd helped him.

Orran wouldn't find out until he actually contacted her, something he was going to do as soon as they were back in the air. She needed to know, and he needed to find out what was happening. He'd tried to contact her earlier, but he hadn't been able to, a sign that she'd been in her human form. Hopefully, the next time he reached out, she would be available. He needed answers, and so did she. He wasn't sure he would *like* those answers, but he would find out sooner rather than later.

CHAPTER FOUR

Now that the shock of flying was over, Blake couldn't deny it felt incredible. He wasn't clutched in Orran's paw anymore, and even though sitting on Orran's back was strange and felt precarious, Blake wouldn't have changed it. He felt oddly safe, and he knew he would miss this once it was over. He didn't know how long it would take before Orran dumped his ass somewhere and headed back home, but he had no doubt it would happen eventually. In the meantime, he would enjoy this as much as he could.

Blue wriggled against his chest, and Blake hugged him more tightly. He rubbed Blue's head with his thumb, not wanting to let go of Orran. It was obvious that dragons weren't made to be ridden, especially not without a saddle. Blake had to hold himself on the protuberances that ran down Orran's back, but they weren't made for that. He wasn't about to let go, though. He didn't fancy splattering on the ground.

He had no idea what would happen when they reached wherever they were going. If he was lucky, Orran wouldn't just abandon him in the forest with no way to go home, and Blake was starting to hope that Orran was a good person who wouldn't do that. They were getting on okay, especially for being a human and a dragon, but he couldn't help but wonder if he would be killed if other dragons found out about this. At the very least, he would probably be jailed, and he wasn't looking forward to it.

It wouldn't be fair. He'd only been trying to help, and he'd succeeded. There was no way to know if Orran and his friends would have been able to get to the egg before Blake's boss did something to it, but Blake suspected it would have been harder for them to retrieve it. This way, they'd gotten it back, and it was safe, or rather, the baby was.

But even though it wouldn't be fair to jail Blake, Blake would understand if that was what happened. Dragons were wary of humans, and they were right to be. Humans could be monsters even to each other, and they considered dragons animals. They didn't know better, but Blake had always thought that people who didn't like animals and who hurt them weren't worth the air they breathed. They should be arrested and pay for what they did, but most people didn't care. They considered animals—all of them, including dragons—inferior, and that wouldn't change. They would have to modify their behavior for it, which was one of the reasons Blake was sure that if anyone found out about dragons being able to become humans, they would freak out and try to kill all the dragons they could get their hands on.

That was why he would never tell anyone about it. If he was ever released, if he ever made his way back to the human world, he would keep his mouth shut. He didn't regret doing the right thing, but he would fight to be free. He hadn't done anything wrong. He'd never hurt dragons or anyone else, and he wasn't planning to.

Of course, that didn't mean dragons would believe him.

He didn't even know if he'd be able to convince them, but he couldn't deny he was curious about dragons, and he was tempted to stay with them if he was allowed to. He had nothing to go back to accept Sheldon, and Sheldon had no place for him in his life.

The baby rubbed against him again, and Blake stroked his back. Blue felt nervous, although Blake might be wrong. He didn't have a lot of experience with babies, since he'd never met his nephews and nieces. His siblings, except for Sheldon, didn't want anything to do with him. That, too, wasn't fair, but there was nothing he could do about it. There might be something he could do about this situation, though, and if that was the case, he would find a way.

He was weak, especially compared to dragons. Orran could have killed him with one thought, and he still could. But he hadn't, and Blake needed to have faith, both in Orran and in himself. He didn't think Orran would allow anyone to hurt him. He might not like Blake much, but he tolerated him, and he knew that Blake had been telling the truth. He was only taking care of the baby. He'd never meant to hurt him, and he still didn't.

But of course, Orran might be the easiest one to convince. He'd been right there when the egg had opened and when the baby had decided that Blake would make a nice tree to climb onto. He had been there to watch Blake take care of Blue. He couldn't deny that was what Blake wanted to do, but anyone else would be able to ignore it. If they didn't take the time to listen, they might burn Blake to a crisp, and he wouldn't be allowed to say a word before dying.

He shook his head. That made him almost lose his balance, and he grabbed at the protuberances, silently berating himself.

He needed to stop thinking about this. He had to focus on Blue and on the future, not on the fact that he might not have one. Whatever happened, he was okay with himself. He might have lost his job, and he might be about to lose his life, but he hadn't looked the other way when someone had needed him. It wasn't much, but it still meant a lot to him. He hoped it would mean a lot to others, too, like Sheldon. Sheldon might never find out what happened to Blake, but Blake hoped he would remember him fondly.

Blue tried to get Blake's attention again, and Blake finally looked down. He had to stop thinking about this. He was worried, and in turn, it clearly worried the baby. Blake wasn't sure how much the baby could feel and experience, but he didn't want to take the risk. If the baby knew how stressed he was, he might freak out, and Blake didn't want that to happen. On instinct, he leaned down and kissed the baby's head. Blue's eyes slid closed and he snuggled closer, pressing his head in the crook of Blake's arm. Blake talked to him, even though he doubted Blue could hear anything. He might be able to feel the vibrations in Blake's chest, though, and it seemed to be enough, because he was asleep only a few minutes later.

Blake looked at the sky. If this was the last freedom he had, he needed to take advantage of it. There wasn't much he could do, but he could look around and feast his eyes on the world. It was more than he'd ever seen, and that he might ever see again. It wasn't a lot, but it was what he had, and he would make do.

He always did.

Your Majesty? Orran called out as soon as he and Blake were in the air.

The last time he'd tried, the queen hadn't answered. It wasn't worrying, not yet, but Orran really needed to talk to her.

Orran? she answered a few minutes later.

Orran huffed in relief. *I wasn't sure I'd be able to reach you.*

You're lucky. I've been spending quite a bit of time in my human form. I had to watch the tapes to see the humans who took my baby. She paused, and Orran waited for her to continue. *How is the egg?*

Orran wasn't looking forward to explaining to her that it had hatched, but he needed to. *The baby was born, Your Majesty.*

Already? They should have had a little more time.

I think what happened rattled them. Him. I'm sorry, Your Majesty. But your egg hatched, and it's a boy.

He's healthy?

He is. Orran also wasn't looking forward to explaining to her that the baby's main care giver was a human, but she needed to know everything. *When I found the egg, a human had it. I had to take both of them when I fled.*

What happened to the human?

He's still with me. Unfortunately, when the egg hatched, the baby latched onto him. I don't think he believes the human is one of his parents, but he does see him as someone who will protect him, and even when I tried to take him away, he didn't want to come. He tried to burn me. The human is trustworthy, though. I made sure of that. I wouldn't allow him to spend time with your heir otherwise.

The laughter coming through the bond startled Orran. He waited for it to end, and he was only mildly surprised when the queen asked, *How have you been dealing with the human?*

As well as I could. He's not what I expected, but then I never thought I would be needing a human.

My baby is already strong if he threatened you. How taken is he with the human?

Enough that I wouldn't want to hurt him by taking him away.

And you truly trust the human?

That was the question, wasn't it? Orran did trust Blake, but what would happen if that trust was broken? He didn't know, but he needed to make a decision. *I trust him,* he told the queen. *I know it's strange, and I'm the first to have a hard time believing it, but Blake had a lot of occasions to hurt both the baby and me, yet he didn't. Instead, I've been watching him, and he's been taking care of the baby. He's been bathing him, feeding him, and making sure he's okay. He's been watching over him when he sleeps.*

There was a pause before the queen answered. *You're right. It is a surprise. I'm glad my baby has someone he trusts, though.*

And Orran was glad that he had someone who could take care of the baby. *We're headed home,* he said.

Not yet.

Orran blinked. *Your Majesty?*

I watched the video of the humans. I couldn't see when or where they came in, but I suspect they had help. It's the only thing that makes sense. They shouldn't have known about the palace to begin with. That means that someone inside opened a door for them, let them in, and told them where to find the nest room.

Orran's heart beat faster. *A traitor.*

Yes. We've been trying to flush them out, but so far, we haven't had any results. I don't want you to bring the baby here until I know who did this and make them pay. I won't put my baby in danger. As long as you trust the human . . .

I do. He has nothing to go back to, but he could easily have tried to run away with the baby. Instead, once he realized I only wanted the best for the baby, he stayed. Orran hesitated. He probably shouldn't be asking this of the queen, but he was tempted to, and he supposed that if he didn't try, he wouldn't get results. *Blake has asked me if he could come back home with me.*

You mean to the palace?

Yes. He doesn't have anything to go back to, and I'm a hundred percent sure he didn't have anything to do with the theft. He hasn't gone into details, but the man he worked for stole the egg, and apparently, he won't hesitate to kill Blake if Blake goes back. Blake is human, and we don't owe him anything, but he did save your egg, and if having done that puts him in danger, I don't think it would be right to send him back.

The queen hummed. *I agree. I don't know if I can trust a human, but I do trust you. If you believe that your human isn't a danger for us, then bring him back with you. I don't want my baby to be traumatized even more than he already has been. He had to hatch without me there. I don't want anything else to happen to him.*

Can I explain what's happening to Blake? Orran wasn't sure why he wanted to be honest with Blake, but he didn't think the reason mattered. If Blake was going to come back to the palace with him, he needed to know how things worked. He needed to know what he was going to face and what was happening.

Tell him as much as you think you can trust him with.

That was a huge sign of trust from the queen. Orran had no doubt that if he'd said he didn't trust Blake, she would have told him to get rid of him. And Orran would have. He was grateful he wouldn't have to, though. He liked Blake, as strange as that was, and he needed his help with the baby, especially since it looked like they were going to have to stay away from the palace for a while.

I wish I could be there with him, the queen murmured.

We'll be back before you can notice we were gone, Orran said even though they both knew it wasn't true.

She chuckled. *I doubt that. I'll let you know what's happening here. How is your team?*

We separated, so I'm alone with the human. I heard from Morven, though, and he and the others are okay. Did Slavin make it home in one piece?

He did, although he didn't know what had happened. You had us worried for a while, Orran.

I apologize. With the human with me, I have to spend a lot of time in my human form.

I understand. I trust you, Orran. Keep my baby safe.

I will.

Even if it was the last thing Orran did. It was his job, his life mission. The baby was the heir to the throne, and he would make sure he made it back alive. It didn't matter if he had to spend time in the forest on his own with a human. He could do this. He'd gone through a lot worse.

Take care of him, the queen said.

I will, Your Majesty.

CHAPTER FIVE

Blake was freezing by the time Orran landed. He didn't want Orran to realize that. He doubted Orran had done it on purpose. He knew Orran wasn't used to dealing with humans, so he probably didn't know how cold Blake would be riding on his back. Either that, or he didn't care, although Blake didn't think that was the case.

Orran might have been antagonistic in the beginning, but it had been because he'd wanted to protect Blue. Now that they'd settled things between them, Blake thought that Orran liked him, or at the very least, that he didn't dislike him. He didn't think Orran would want him to suffer on purpose, which was why he believed that Orran just wasn't aware of how uncomfortable riding him was.

Orran shifted almost as soon as Blake was off his back. Blake looked away, not wanting to make Orran uncomfortable by staring. No matter how many times he saw Orran's body, he couldn't help but be fascinated by it. The last thing he wanted was to make an enemy out of Orran, though, and he still didn't know much about dragons, not nearly enough about them or Orran to know if Orran will be offended by him staring.

Probably. Blake would be if someone was looking at him, but then, it would be different.

"I'll take care of the fire," Orran said.

Blake shivered. "Thank you." He could have kissed Orran for thinking about a fire, but he didn't. He liked his balls where they were, as well as his limbs.

"I'll hunt as soon as this is done," Orran said. "I'll shift again, so if you need me to answer anything, you need to ask now."

Blake shook his head. "I'm fine. I'll take care of Blue. Then I'll set him next to the fire." He wasn't looking forward to the night. He'd been freezing last night, and from the sky, he suspected it was going to rain. Blue wouldn't be a problem, not if Blake wrapped him in his jacket, but Blake would freeze.

He didn't have a choice, though. He wasn't going to let Blue be cold just because he couldn't stand it.

Orran shifted, and just like he'd said, he took care of the fire. He'd gathered some wood, and it only took one breath out of him to light it on fire. It was handy to have a dragon along, both for the food and the fire, and Blake sat next to it, stroking Blue's back. The dragon cooed, then tried to follow Orran, but Blake caught him. He raised the baby, wondering how long it would be before he couldn't anymore. "You can't go with him," he scolded. "It's too dangerous."

Blue didn't look happy, but to Blake's relief, the baby dragon got distracted after he noticed a fly passing by. He ran after it, and Blake watched him, smiling. Once he was sure Blue wasn't going to try to sneak after Orran, he reached for his phone in his pocket.

He'd had it in his pocket when Orran had taken him, but it was off, of course. Now the battery had run out, and it wasn't useful to Blake, but it helped him remember his life.

He hadn't liked it. Hell, he'd hated it and the way his family had treated him. It wasn't like he'd done anything bad. He liked men and hadn't been able to find a good job. He'd been unlucky, and yes, in the beginning, it had certainly been his fault. He hadn't been as serious as he should have been. Still, he knew that the main reason his family didn't want him around was his sexuality, and he hated that, especially since he was pretty sure that Sheldon wasn't all that straight either.

But Sheldon had never come out to their parents, and he probably wouldn't. He knew he couldn't if he wanted to keep them in his life.

Blake wished he could call his brother. He missed him, even though he knew it was best for everyone. He just wanted to tell Sheldon that he was okay. He didn't want Sheldon to worry, which he would inevitably do, even though they weren't close. Sheldon was a worrier, and he would want to know what had happened to Blake.

Blake kept an eye on the baby after putting his phone back into his pocket. Blue didn't go far. Instead, he was trying to take flight but not managing, and when Orran came back with a bloody carcass, Blake snatched the baby and held him close. "I hope you're not planning on having me cook that thing?" he asked.

Orran rolled his eyes as an answer. Blake had found that he and Orran could communicate pretty well, even when Orran was in his dragon form. It wasn't easy, but Orran's face was very expressive. The rolling eyes meant that of course he hadn't expected Blake to take care of this. Hell, he probably thought Blake couldn't do it, and he wouldn't be wrong. Blake liked meat, but usually, he bought it in the supermarket. He'd never hunted in his life, and he wasn't about to start. He would rather eat grass.

Orran took care of everything, from cleaning the meat to cooking it, while Blake focused on the baby. Once the baby had eaten, he curled into Blake's lap and went to sleep, and Blake had to stifle a yawn. He wasn't sure why he was so tired since he hadn't done anything except sitting on Orran's back, but that was the reality of it. He was probably in mild shock or something like that after everything he'd been through.

Blake sighed. With the baby in his lap already sleeping, he could settle down for the night, too. It had started drizzling while they were eating, and even though they were under trees, it didn't keep away all of the rain. Blake didn't want Blue to get cold or wet, so he took off his jacket and put it on the baby, bundling him into it. Blue didn't wake up, and Blake stretched onto his side, holding the bundle of jacket and dragon against his chest. At the very least, that part of his body would be warm.

"Good night," he told Orran.

Orran was once again in his dragon form, and he nodded at Blake.

Blake closed his eyes and tried to go to sleep. Of course, that was when the rain started coming down more heavily. Blake curled himself tighter around Blue, hoping to keep the baby dry but knowing it wouldn't be possible.

It took him a moment to realize that even though the rain was coming down harder now, he wasn't getting wet. He could feel the dampness in the air, but the water wasn't reaching him, and it had been a few moments earlier.

He opened his eyes.

He jerked back when he saw what stood above him, then sucked in a breath when he realized what was happening.

Orran had moved closer. He was next to Blake now, and he'd extended his wing over him. He was shielding Blake and Blue from the water, and when Blake looked at his face, he rolled his eyes again.

Blake bit his lower lips. "Thank you."

Orran shrugged, which was a sight when he was in his dragon form. He tucked his wing closer to his body, dragging Blake closer, and the night disappeared around Blake. Everything was dark now, and he was already starting to feel warmer.

He didn't know how Orran would react, but he pressed closer to his side, burying his face against it. He felt Orran shudder, but he didn't know if it was because of the contact or because of the cold. Orran stopped moving, though, and

Blake didn't dare ask him what was going on. Orran wouldn't be able to answer him anyway, and Blake wasn't sure he wanted an answer.

Orran had to be doing this for Blue. It was the only thing that made sense, but even if that was the case, it didn't matter. Blake gently rubbed Orran's side and murmured, "Thank you."

Then he closed his eyes and let sleep claim him.

CHAPTER SIX

When Blake woke up, Orran was wrapped around him. He didn't realize what was happening at first, and he blinked, staring at the top of Blue's head. Blue was still asleep, curled into Blake's arms, and Blake tightened his hold on him. Blue grumbled, but he didn't wake up.

Then, Blake started to realize what was happening *behind* him.

When he'd fallen asleep, Orran had been next to him, in his dragon form. He'd used his wing to shield Blake and Blue from the rain and the coldness of the night, but somehow, he'd shifted in his sleep, and he was now very much human. Blake could feel it.

He could feel a lot of things, including Orran's arm that was hooked around his waist.

He had no idea what to do. While he had admired Orran's naked form, and he had to admit that he liked the man, this was a new situation for them. They still didn't fully trust each other, but now they were sleeping together.

Not in the way Blake wished they were, though.

He could feel his cheeks heating, and he knew he had to get out of the situation. Not only was Orran plastered against him, spooning him, but Blake could also feel something hard poking him in the ass.

So, Orran had a cock after all.

Blake was *not* going to examine how that made him feel, not right now. He couldn't help but wonder for a split second where that cock had come from, but he pushed the thought away as fast as it had come to him. He needed to get out of Orran's arms, and he wasn't sure how. In spite of whatever it was he could feel, he doubted Orran was attracted to him. He had shown no sign of it, and this surely had more to do with nature than with the way Orran felt about him. Blake was already embarrassed enough. He didn't want Orran to be aware of what was happening right now.

His problem was that Blue was in his arms. If he moved, he would wake the baby dragon, and that was the last thing he wanted. Still, that had to be better than waiting for Orran to wake up and realize what was going on.

He decided that wiggling down would be the best thing. As soon as he was out of Orran's arms, he could sit up at the very least. He held his breath, then inched downward.

It felt like an eternity had passed before he made any progress, and of course, that was when Blue woke up.

The baby dragon opened one eye and chirped at Blake. Blake froze, holding his breath. When Blue chirped at him again, he shushed him. "Don't wake Orran up," he murmured.

Of course, that only made Blue chirp louder. He wriggled until Blake had to let him go, then hopped out of Blake's arms and roared. Blake winced. He didn't know why Blue was behaving like that, and he didn't think it mattered, not at this point.

"He's making too much noise," Orran said.

Blake didn't know what to do. He was still half in Orran's arms, and he expected the dragon to say something about it. Instead, Orran rolled to his back and sat up. He rubbed his face, and for one moment, he looked adorable. His blue hair was tangled, and he had a mark on his cheek. Blake allowed himself to imagine how it would be to wake up next to him in a bed, not frantically trying to get away from him, but instead, laying there until he opened his eyes. Then, they would kiss, and —

Shit. Blake needed to stop that. "Good morning," he said in a strangled voice.

Orran got to his feet and stretched, and Blake had to look away. "Good morning. What's going on with Blue?"

"I don't know. You're the dragon. You tell me."

Orran crouched and held a hand out to Blue. Blue didn't trust him, so he didn't move closer. Instead, he put himself behind Blake, climbing on top of him until he was on his shoulder. He wacked Blake in the face with his tail, and Blake decided that was enough.

He took the baby and put him back on the ground, then got to his feet. His entire body was tense, and he felt like his back might break if he slept another night on the ground. He wasn't that old, but he felt like he was eighty.

"I think he's hungry," Blake told Orran. He peeked at him, and just like always, Orran's body caught his attention. At least he wasn't at groin level anymore.

There was nothing to be seen at Orran's groin, just like there hadn't been yesterday. Blake knew what he'd felt, though, and he tried to get a better look without giving himself away and without looking like a creep. He suspected that Orran did have a cock, and that said cock was hidden in the pouch at Orran's groin. It had a slit, but since Blake had been avoiding looking at it, he hadn't thought about what it could be. Now, it was kind of obvious.

But that wasn't the most impressive thing about Orran's body. He was gorgeous all around. His long flowing hair, his strange eyes, the blue patches of scales on his skin — all of that appealed to Blake, and he wanted to run his fingers over the scales, to find out how they felt. He wanted to stroke the skin of Orran's stomach to see if he was ticklish. He wanted to feel Orran's claws on his own flesh, knowing that Orran wouldn't hurt him.

Or maybe he would if he caught Blake staring at him the way he was. The fact that he didn't seem to care about nudity didn't mean he would take Blake ogling him well.

Blake cleared his throat. "Thank you," he said. His voice was slightly rough, and he hoped Orran wouldn't realize why that was.

Orran cocked his head. "What are you thanking me for?"

"For shielding me last night. I slept better because I wasn't as cold."

"You were cold?"

"The first night, yes. I'm not used to sleeping under the stars, and I can't say that the ground is the most comfortable bed I've ever had. But having you close helped. You're very . . .warm." Orran ran *hot*, and Blake truly hadn't been cold after he'd pressed himself against him. Even more so this morning, when *Orran* had been pressing against him.

Blake didn't understand why he was attracted to Orran, but he didn't think it mattered. Attraction wasn't something anyone could understand. Blake was usually attracted to guys shorter than him, slimmer, and while Orran was on the slight side, he was also tall and strong. His appearance was odd, at least to Blake's eyes, but Blake liked what he knew of Orran. He was protective and honest. He could have killed Blake or abandoned him, but instead, he'd listened to him, and he'd allowed him to stay with him and Blue. He took care of the baby, even though it was obvious he was awkward with him. But Blake wasn't afraid of leaving Blue with Orran anymore, and he knew that he needed to keep himself in check. He had no idea what Orran felt for him or what he thought about him. He couldn't risk Orran hating him and stomping all over his heart if he found out Blake was attracted to him.

"I'm going to look around and make sure we're still alone," Orran said.

Blake looked away and nodded. "Yes, thank you. I'm

pretty sure Blue is hungry."

"You already said that."

Blake tended to repeat himself when he was nervous, so he wasn't surprised. "Yes, well, it hasn't changed. The baby is still hungry. You should go while I feed him."

Orran was looking at him as if he couldn't understand him, and Blake suspected he truly couldn't. That was okay. At least he wasn't as transparent as he thought.

He hoped so, anyway.

Blake was acting weird. Orran was pretty sure the reason he thought Blake was weird was that he didn't understand humans, but he couldn't be sure, and it was worrying him. What if Blake was planning something? Orran didn't think so, but he didn't trust himself when it came to humans, especially Blake. For whatever reason, he was getting attached to this human in particular, and he knew that would influence the way he felt about him.

He needed to be more careful.

He didn't hate Blake. He'd thought he would, considering what humans did to dragons, and he was surprised to find that his feelings were very different. He shouldn't like Blake, yet he did. He found Blake appealing. His body was strange, but he was a good person, and even though Orran had been reluctant, Blake had forced him to see that not all humans wanted to hurt dragons.

He supposed that some humans were afraid of dragons the same way dragons were afraid of them. Blake probably shared some of Orran's feelings when he thought of dragons — terrified, worried, angry. But Blake had been nice, both to Orran and Blue. He hadn't tried to hurt either of them, and Orran didn't think he would.

It was odd for him to accept that, and to admit that even

though Blake was human, he wasn't dangerous. Orran was more dangerous to him than he was to Orran. He could hurt Blake with one flick of his tail, one breath of fire. What could Blake do to him?

Orran suspected that if he allowed it, Blake could hurt him in other ways. He didn't know what to think about that, but he realized now wasn't the right moment to focus on it. Instead, he finished checking the forest around the spot where they'd spent the night. Then he went back to Blake and Blue.

Blue was eating when Orran landed, and he chirped at him, his mouth full. Orran huffed in amusement, then shifted. The transformation in Blake was instant. He'd been smiling as he looked from Orran to Blue, but as soon as Orran was in his human form, his gaze shifted, and he didn't look back.

It was one more thing Orran didn't understand about Blake.

Orran settled by the fire, crossing his legs. When he reached for a piece of meat, Blake wiggled until he was sitting further away from Orran than he had been before. He tsked at the sight of Blue toppled on his back, playing with his tail. "Don't play while you're eating," he gently scolded.

Orran had to work hard not to smile. Blake was behaving like a father, which was surprising. Blue hadn't yet shifted to his human form, and there was no way for Orran to find out when he would. It was too soon—it would be at least a few months, probably more. The queen had been precocious as a child, but that didn't mean her son would be. Yet Blake was treating him as he would a human baby.

Orran stayed silent, trying to read Blake and to find out why he was behaving weirdly. Now that he had a human with him, he wished he'd paid more attention to the humans he'd met. Of course, he'd killed most of those, so it probably wasn't the same. Blake was nothing like those humans. If Orran had to guess, he doubted Blake had ever hurt anyone in his life, and it made Orran feel better. It was ridiculous, but Orran couldn't help it.

"How long will it be until we arrive?" Blake asked.

Orran blinked. He'd been thinking about Blake, but he hadn't been listening to him. "I'm sorry?"

"To wherever we're going. I know you said we had to go slow because Blue gets tired easily and needs to eat often, but I was wondering how long it was going to take us."

Orran hesitated. The queen had told him he could tell Blake whatever he needed to know, including news about the traitor. Orran hadn't yet, and he wasn't a hundred percent sure he should. Still, Blake had questions, and he deserved to know. If he was going to stick with them, if he was going to move to the palace, then he ought to know what kind of situation he was getting himself into.

Orran straightened. "I talked to the queen yesterday," he announced.

Blake's eyes widened. "What? The queen?"

"Blue's mother. I had something to tell her."

"Do I have anything to do with that?"

"You know you do."

"Well? What did she say? Do you have to dump me in the forest? Kill me? Is Blue a prince, then?"

Orran cocked his head. "Aren't you afraid I might do just that?" He didn't look or sound afraid.

Blake hesitated. He bit his lower lip in a gesture that appealed to Orran, and Orran found himself leaning closer. Luckily, he realized it, and he moved back, hoping Blake hadn't noticed. Orran already had enough trouble understanding how he felt. He didn't need Blake to ask about that, too.

"Are you going to do it?" Blake asked.

Dammit. Orran had been distracted again. "Do what?"

"Kill me? Is that what the queen told you to do?"

Orran shook his head. He didn't want Blake to panic. "She didn't. It's the opposite. I told her about you and how you protected Blue. I told her how her son clung to you and tried to protect you. She agreed that you should come back to the palace with us."

Blake sucked in a breath. "Really?"

Orran nodded. "Really. I'll explain what you'll find when you get there so you don't get scared."

"Why should I be scared? This is *incredible*."

Blake might not believe he would be scared, but Orran knew that wasn't the truth. He was human, and he'd freaked out at the sight of one dragon landing in front of him. The palace was full of them, and most stayed in their dragon form most of the time. Others, especially the younger ones, would no doubt shift to have conversations with Blake, especially since he was physically appealing and a nice man, but Orran doubted the older ones would. They'd stay away and would be suspicious.

That was okay. As long as they didn't hurt Blake, Orran didn't care what they thought about him. But Blake needed to be aware of the traitor. He had to know why they were wasting time in the forest.

Orran cleared his throat. "The queen said she doesn't want us to go back to the palace yet."

Blake frowned. "Why not? I would have thought she would be eager to see her son."

"You mean to meet him. Remember, he hadn't hatched when he was taken. She only knows him as an egg."

Blake's expression twisted. "That has to be horrible. We should get her son to her as soon as possible."

Would Blake ever stop surprising Orran? Orran doubted that, and he was grateful for it. He *enjoyed* it. "She wants us to stay in the forest for a while longer. She suspects there's a traitor in the palace."

Blake looked at Blue, but the baby dragon was chasing his tail again, and he wasn't listening to them. "Can you explain?"

"You know the egg was stolen from the palace. The queen laid it in the egg room, and it shouldn't have been possible for humans to get to it or to enter the palace. Yet we have proof they did. We have video cameras, and they filmed everything. As far as I know, no dragon is visible with the humans, but it would be impossible for them to know where the egg room is. They shouldn't even be aware of the palace, yet they found it and managed to sneak in without anyone noticing and without breaking in. They didn't linger but went straight to the egg room. That means they had to have had inside help."

Blake whistled. "That's bad. Does the queen know who it is?"

"Not yet, but I'm sure she has suspicions." She would no doubt look at her family and the dragons who had an eye on the throne and would be eager to step into her place if she didn't produce an heir, and worse, if word went around that humans had stolen her egg. "We need to wait for her to tell us we can go back."

Blake peered at Blue. "I guess it could be worse." He frowned. "Unless you're going to make me sleep under the rain?"

Orran couldn't blush. He never did. His cheeks felt warm for a different reason. It was the only thing that made sense — the only thing Orran would admit. "I'll cover you and Blue with my wing from now on. You should have told me about that yesterday. I would have made sure the baby wasn't cold."

Blake grinned at him. "And you say you don't care about me."

Orran shook his head. "I care about the baby."

"Sure you do. Keep telling yourself that."

That was *precisely* what Orran was going to do. It wasn't the right moment for him to deal with whatever feelings he had for Blake, no matter how irresistible Blake was.

Blake wasn't surprised to find out about the traitor now that he knew the entire story. It made sense. How else could humans have snuck into a palace? No one even knew it existed, which meant someone had told them about it. Who better than a dragon who lived there?

It had to be hard for Orran to wrap his mind around it. He trusted his people. And that trust had been betrayed, and he and his people had almost lost a baby. Blake could too easily imagine what would have happened to Blue if he were still in his boss's hands.

Once again, Blake was glad he'd decided to take the egg and run away. He might have put himself in trouble, but he'd saved a life, and that was enough for him. He wanted to keep Blue safe. That was his main goal since he'd found the egg, and it hadn't changed.

"So we take our time," he said.

Orran nodded. "At least until the queen tells me we can go back. I don't know how long it's going to take her to find the traitor."

Blake bit his lower lip. "When you say the queen, you mean an actual queen?" He had noticed that earlier, but he hadn't wanted to interrupt.

Orran paled for a second. Then, he visibly shook himself and nodded. "I do mean a queen the way humans think about queens and kings. Of course, she doesn't have as many subjects as you're used to. She's the queen of our clan, the Ogorth clan. She's our leader. Her family always has been."

"And someone stole her egg."

"Exactly."

That probably meant that whoever had done it was trying to take over the clan. Blake might not know much about dragons and how their society worked, but that much, he could tell. "Does she have any idea who could have done this?"

"I don't know. She hasn't told me. She wants me to focus on Blue, and I agreed."

"Good. We can take care of him together. We'll make sure nothing happens to him, and you'll get him back to his mother in one piece and good health." Orran did that thing where he cocked his head and looked at Blake. Blake ignored him. He didn't know what Orran was trying to understand, and it didn't matter. "When you say we need to waste time, you don't mean we're going to stay in one place all that time, right?" he asked.

"We can't. I don't know if the humans are still hunting us, but we can't risk it. I need to contact the rest of my team."

"So do it."

"I will, once we're in the air. Make sure the baby has eaten and rested. We'll fly away as soon as possible."

Blake knew that was the end of the conversation. He didn't mind. He had a lot of things to think about, like the tidbit that he apparently was going to live with the clan of dragons in their palace. What did that even mean? Did Orran mean *palace* the way Blake and humans generally did? Or was it just an enormous cave or something? Blake didn't know how dragons lived. He wanted to find out, though. He wasn't sure he cared if there was running water or electricity. He could do without.

Well, at least for a bit.

He packed up their stuff, which wasn't much, then held his hands out to Blue. The baby clambered up Blake's thighs, hooking his claws in Blake's jeans. Blake winced, hoping the baby wouldn't make holes in them. He didn't exactly have a change of clothes.

He was getting pretty ripe. He wanted to take a bath, although he wasn't sure it was a good idea. He didn't even have clean clothes to put back on. Still, he could ask. He turned to Orran, smiling when he saw that Orran was still in his human form. "Hey, can we stop near a body of water next time?"

Orran blinked. "Of course. Why do you ask?"

"I'd like to take a bath, and I'm pretty sure Blue could use one, too."

"I see. Yes, it can be done."

"Thanks." Blake suspected it wasn't great to be next to him right now, not with the stench that emanated from him. He didn't apologize for it, though. There was nothing he could do about it. He hadn't showered in two days, and he was still wearing the same clothes he'd had on when he went to work three days earlier. He couldn't change the situation. Hopefully, a bath would help more than doing nothing.

Once they were ready, Orran shifted. Blake had been a bit wary of looking at his dragon body, just like he'd tried not to stare at his human body. Now, though, he took his time admiring him. He knew Orran wouldn't mind, not if the rolling of his eyes meant anything. "Can I touch you?" he asked.

Orran hesitated, then nodded. Blue chirped from his perch on Blake's shoulder, and Blake rubbed the top of his head before stroking a hand along Orran's side.

He'd slept against it. He'd slept against *Orran*, cuddled next to him, and he hadn't thought anything of it. He still didn't.

He couldn't believe humans thought of dragons as animals. He supposed that at first sight, they were. The dark blue of Orran's scales glinted in the sunlight, and dust rose every time he took a step. He huffed, and a plume of smoke escaped his nostrils. It made Blake laugh, and Blue made a strange sound, almost as if he were laughing, too.

Orran wasn't an animal, and neither was Blue. They might

be able to transform into dragons, but it didn't change the fact that they were as human as Blake, or that they were beautiful.

Blake shouldn't go down that path, though. He might find Orran beautiful in both his forms, and he might be moving in with the clan, but it didn't mean anything would come out of whatever he and Orran had going on. Maybe they were too different. Maybe humans had hurt dragons too much for Orran to be able to see Blake in another light. He seemed to have accepted Blake's presence, but it didn't mean he was happy to have him here, or that he'd want anything to do with him in an intimate situation.

Blake dropped his hand and took a step back. He didn't miss the way Orran looked at him, but he kept his gaze on what he was doing as he climbed onto Orran's back.

It was probably stupid of him to think that Orran could see him that way. Hell, he didn't even know if dragons had the same kind of relationships humans had, or if Orran liked female dragons rather than males. He didn't know anything about Orran, not when it came to his private life, and it was probably better that way. He could see himself falling in love with Orran, unfortunately. Orran was strong and gentle. He wanted the best for Blue and for their clan. He was protective, and he was starting to trust Blake. Blake loved that, and he didn't want to risk it, especially not to get his dick wet.

But it wasn't just that, was it? He could admit it, at least to himself. He found Orran incredibly attractive, that much was true. But he was starting to have feelings for him, and he doubted they would change. They wouldn't fade, that was for sure. If they did change, they would become stronger, and Blake would be in trouble. He didn't even know if Orran had someone waiting for him at home, a beautiful dragon lady who would carry his eggs and give him a family.

Blake needed to stop thinking about it.

He patted Orran's neck. "We're ready," he said, clutching

Blue to his chest.

Orran twisted his neck to look at him, and Blake forced himself to smile. He didn't want Orran to realize something was up. Luckily for him, Orran couldn't ask what was going on, so he nodded, then took flight.

Blake closed his eyes. He had the length of this flight to manage to get Orran out of his thoughts. He needed to make it happen so that he'd be okay when they landed.

He wasn't sure he could.

CHAPTER SEVEN

The only news Orran had by the time they landed was what he'd gotten from Morven. They'd managed to ditch the humans, but Morven was pretty sure they were still looking, and he suspected at least some of them had gone after Orran. Orran didn't like that. He and Blake hadn't seen anyone, but he knew humans could be sneaky when they wanted to be, and they had a lot to gain if they caught up to Orran, Blake, and Blue. Orran couldn't allow that to happen, but he was just one dragon. He would fight as much as he had to if the time came, but depending on how many humans there were, he might lose both his life and Blue.

He didn't want to think about that, though. He'd decided to go toward the palace, just in case he and Blake needed to make a quick escape. He wasn't too close, so the traitor probably wouldn't know they were there, but close enough to fly home if he needed to. There was a body of water there, just like Blake had asked, and Orran found himself smiling at the human's reaction when they landed.

"This is incredible," Blake said. There was awe in his voice, and Orran knew he meant it.

He'd always thought humans didn't care about the beauty of nature. Of course, that might still be the case. He was starting to realize that Blake wasn't a normal human. He didn't want to hurt dragons. He didn't want to hurt anyone, not unless he was forced. He wanted to take care of people instead, and he had. He was the main reason Blue was safe and happy right now.

Orran could too easily imagine what would have happened if the egg had hatched with only him present. He would have taken care of Blue as much as he could, of course, and he would have made sure Blue was safe, but he knew the baby would have missed something. Blake was paternal with him, and it wasn't something Orran could have done. Watching Blake and Blue together made him wonder if Blake would eventually become a father. Probably. It suited him, but the thought of Blake having a baby with someone else, with a human woman, made Orran want to tear something apart. It didn't make sense, and he refused to examine those feelings too closely. Now wasn't the time.

Blake looked up from Blue. "Any news from the palace?" he asked.

Orran shook his head, grateful for the distraction. "I haven't heard anything from the queen, but I did contact the rest of my team."

"And?"

"They managed to leave the humans behind, but Morven suspects some of them are after us."

Blake's expression hardened. "I'm not surprised. They're going to want to take Blue back, and if they can get you in the process, they won't hesitate."

"Are you aware of what will happen to us if they catch up to us?"

Blake's expression shifted again. Orran was amazed at how easily he could read the human. Maybe it was because they'd been spending time together, or maybe because Blake was open with him. "I know *exactly* what will happen to you and Blue if they get their hands on you. That's why I won't let it happen."

Orran snorted before he could stop himself. "What can you do against a group of humans?"

"Probably not as much as you, but it's not going to stop me

from trying. Do you really think I'll let them hurt you if there's something I can do?"

Orran didn't. He knew Blake well enough by now. "I don't."

Blake nodded once. "Exactly. I might not do any good, but I'll do everything I can anyway. I won't let them take you or hurt you."

Orran didn't want to think about this anymore. He didn't want to think about the fierceness in Blake's voice, about how it was almost as if he cared about Orran as much as he cared for Blue.

He looked toward the lake and cleared his throat. "You said you wanted a bath?"

Blake blinked, no doubt at the abrupt change in conversation. "I did. I'm not sure how much good it's going to do, since I don't have clean clothes, but I suppose I'll find out." He hesitated. "Thank you."

"You have nothing to thank me for. You said you wanted to give the baby a bath. That's why I chose this spot."

To Orran's surprise, the corner of Blake's lips curled into a smile. "Sure. That's why you did it. Not because you wanted me to have something I asked for." He reached for Blue, who was on his shoulder, and he gently pulled him away, handing him to Orran. "Take care of him for a while, okay?"

Orran wasn't sure how to do that. "I'll hurt him."

Blake laughed. "I don't think so. If *I* didn't hurt him, you won't, either. You know what he needs and what shouldn't be done to him. I had no idea about any of that, yet I managed. Come on. It'll only be for ten minutes. I promise to be back as soon as I'm clean."

Orran couldn't say no. He didn't *want* to say no. He wanted Blake to have this, and anything else he might want.

Blake was right. Orran had done this because he wanted him to be happy. Orran had no idea what it meant, or rather,

81

he suspected he knew what it meant, but it wasn't possible.

How could he have never found a dragon that was appealing enough to him that he'd want something serious with them, yet the first time he met a human, the first time he got close to a human he wasn't planning to kill, he wanted to give him the moon? He didn't have an answer to that. He supposed that feelings didn't have answers or reasons. Still, it was inconvenient, to say the least.

He cradled Blue to his chest as Blake left them behind. He couldn't avoid looking at Blake as he walked away, and he couldn't deny the human was appealing. He was different from dragons, but that didn't make him less beautiful. He was stockier, his body less graceful, but he gave Orran a sense of protection, even though Orran was aware that he could stomp the life out of Blake with one movement.

He wouldn't. He'd begun to care for Blake, even though it didn't make sense. He was grateful the queen had agreed to have Blake move into the palace, at least for a while. It would take Orran some time to get used to a life without him again, even though they'd only been together for a few days.

He was in trouble.

He needed to do something to distract himself, so he put Blue down as soon as Blake was out of sight. Blue couldn't seem to stay still. He ran after a butterfly, then tried to sneak away to get back to Blake, crying out for him. Orran did the best he could, keeping him close as soon as he realized what was happening, but Blue was having none of that. He tried to burn Orran a few times, then finally, he managed to escape, sneaking behind a tree while Orran was busy with the fire.

Blue half ran, half flew, toward the lake, and Orran went after him in his human form. He stumbled, almost falling on his face, but he managed to get his hands on the baby dragon. He raised him to his face, turning him around so they could look at each other. "Don't do that," he said, a growl in his voice. "You need to stay close. He's going to come back, I promise."

A splash caught Orran's attention, and he looked up.

That was a mistake.

Orran hadn't realized how close they'd come to the lake, and from where he was, he had a perfect view of Blake. The human was entirely naked, and Orran didn't even try to stop his gaze from moving over his entire body and to his groin.

Blake had been right. They were *very* different in that area, yet also not much. Blake had a cock, but it wasn't hidden like Orran's was. His skin was entirely pink, redder now than it usually was, probably because of the cold water. His hair was wet and dripped over his shoulders, drops of water sliding down his skin. There was hair on his chest, down his stomach, and around his soft cock, and Orran's hands itched to touch it. He didn't have hair except on his head, and he wondered how it felt.

He wouldn't find out. He should go back to the encampment, give Blake some privacy, but he couldn't seem to be able to move.

Blake knew Orran was watching him. He'd heard the dragon coming from afar. He hadn't been discreet, and neither had Blue. Blake was surprised Blue couldn't even give him the time to take a bath on his own, but maybe he shouldn't be. For all that Blue was a dragon, he was still a newborn, and he needed to be with someone twenty-four seven. Apparently, that someone was Blake. It wasn't a problem for him, and next time, he would make sure to take Blue with him when he bathed. The situation had had a surprising resolution, though. Orran had managed to catch Blue, and now, he was standing there, staring at Blake.

Blake didn't mind. Knowing he was being watched was

thrilling, and he decided to take his time. It was obvious Orran was interested in him, or at the very least, in his body. Maybe he was only mystified by it. Maybe he didn't understand it, and he wanted to. Maybe he wanted to look at the differences between them. Whatever the reason, Blake didn't mind. He also hoped that maybe the reason Orran was watching him was that he liked what he was seeing and that he was attracted to it.

The situation couldn't last forever, though. The water was freezing, and while Blake made sure to wash every nook and cranny he could get to, he knew he couldn't stay in there for much longer. He was longing for the fire, and he was shivering by the time he got out. When he looked up, Orran was gone. Blake hadn't heard him walk away, but he was grateful he wouldn't have to face him.

He expected Orran to say something when he got back to the encampment, but instead, the dragon was focused on Blue, who was in his lap. He looked up and smiled when he heard Blake, but that was it. Blake wasn't about to bring it up, either. He knew Orran had seen him. He didn't know what it meant, but he would eventually find out.

He settled next to the fire and gestured toward the lake. "You should go get a bath, too."

"Dinner is almost ready," Orran answered without looking at Blake.

"It's fine. I'll keep an eye on it. You could take Blue with you. I'm sure you know more than me about cleaning dragons and giving them baths."

Orran looked slightly terrified at the thought of bathing Blue, but Blake ignored it. He didn't know if Blue and Orran would have a relationship once they got to the palace, but for now, Orran was in charge of the baby just as much as Blake was. He needed to learn to deal with him.

No matter how much Blake wanted to sneak around and

look at the two dragons in the water, he didn't. He sat right where he was and listened to them. They weren't quiet, especially Blue, who seemed to be having a lot of fun in the water. He probably couldn't feel the cold in dragon form, and it made Blake smile—and slightly jealous. He'd never wished he were a dragon, but now, he did a bit. That was probably because he hadn't known dragons could transform into humans before. He hadn't wanted to be an animal.

But dragons weren't animals, were they? They had a human side, and *Orran's* human side was gorgeous and appealing. Blake didn't know what would happen between them, but for the first time since Orran had grabbed him in the alley, he was starting to wonder if there could be something.

He didn't know how other dragons would take it. He didn't even know if Orran would be interested in him, since he was male. He thought that was the case, though. But what if dragons didn't accept same-sex couples? What if they didn't want Blake to stay because he was human? He would never ask Orran to choose. No one should have to make that kind of decision.

Blake was getting ahead of himself. They weren't even at the palace yet, so he shouldn't start thinking that way. Maybe he would be surprised. Maybe the dragons would be welcoming.

He snorted at himself. Even if some were, he already knew most wouldn't be. They feared humans, and they were right to. Humans were assholes.

He was grateful when Orran and Blue came back. It was a distraction he welcomed, and he opened his arms to cuddle the baby against his chest. Blue was still damp, and he was clearly tired. Blake stroked his back as he ate, and he made sure that Blue had eaten enough before he finally fell asleep in his slap.

Blake never stopped touching him even as he ate himself.

He could feel Orran's gaze on him, but he wasn't troubled by it. Orran always took time to think before he asked questions, so he wasn't surprised when after a while, Orran asked, "Why do you want to come to the palace?"

"I already told you. I don't have anything to go back to in the city."

"But you know that life. Even though you don't have a family, you know the city and the humans. At the palace, though, you won't know anyone. Everyone will be different from you. You could get hurt so easily. Aren't you afraid?"

"I'm *terrified*. I know how much dragons hate humans, and I don't blame them. I hope they won't hate me just because I'm human, but I know better than to think that hate is rational. So yes. I'm afraid. I'm also eager, though. You don't know how incredible this is for me. I've always been fascinated by dragons, and I am even more now that I know you have a human side. I want to find out about you. I want to get to know you."

Orran blinked. "You mean me in particular?"

Blake laughed. "Yes, you. And Blue, and Blue's mother. I want to find out about your life at the palace. I want to know what you do for the queen, why you were the one who came after her baby."

"Would you tell me about your own life?"

Blake shrugged. "If you want, sure. There's not a lot to say, though. You already know most of it. I had a shit job, and I worked for the wrong person."

"But *you* are a good person, aren't you?"

Blake rubbed the back of his neck. "I don't know. I like to think I do good things. But are people really good or bad? Besides, there isn't much to me. I had a job, but it's not like I have money or even a home or a family."

"Being a good person is more important than being rich."

"It is," Blake agreed. "Money would make my life easier,

though. It's hard to sleep at night when you don't know where your next paycheck is going to come from. It's hard when you go to sleep on an empty stomach because you didn't have money to buy food."

"That bad?" Orran asked softly.

Blake had to look away. "Yeah, pretty much. It's one of the reasons my family wants nothing to do with me."

"I don't understand that. Dragons all live together in the palace. We're close. Even if we're not related, we're still family. Why doesn't your family want you?"

Blake didn't want to talk about this, but he was relieved Orran was asking questions. He was curious about him, which meant he was interested. "They don't like that I'm gay."

"Gay?"

Blake and Orran spoke the same language, so Blake had thought Orran would know what he meant. "You know. I like people of the same sex. Men."

"I see. I heard that word before, but I wasn't sure what it meant. Do humans usually only like the opposite sex?"

"I guess most humans do."

"But why is liking the same sex a bad thing?"

Blake laughed. "I don't have the answer to that. You should ask my family. It's the reason they kicked me out when I was eighteen. I came out to them, and they didn't want anything to do with me. The fact that I wasn't able to find a good job and that I didn't go to college only settled their thought that I would never do anything with my life."

Blake had hated them for that, and he still did, sometimes. But most of the time, he missed having a family, and he suspected that was why he was happy to go with Blake and Blue. Even if the other dragons hated him, he would still have them. They were kind of his family, even though he knew he didn't deserve them.

Orran's heart broke for Blake. He could tell how much being rejected by his own family had hurt Blake. It was obvious in every single word he said, in the way he looked away from Orran as if ashamed.

There was nothing to be ashamed of. Orran wasn't sure that saying that out loud would help, but he wanted to try. "Dragons aren't gay like you said," he started.

Blake bit his lower lip. "Does it mean that all dragons like the other sex?"

Orran shook his head. "That's not what I was trying to say. It's hard to explain, though."

"Try me. I know I'm only human, but it doesn't mean I'm stupid."

There was no heat in Blake's words, but Orran was offended on his behalf. "I never said you were stupid, and I don't think you are. But it's obvious that humans think differently than dragons. You talk about gay and — and this kind of thing as if people can choose."

"It's not, but most humans are straight, which means they like the opposite sex. Then, there's a small percentage of us who like the same sex, the opposite sex *and* the same sex, or who just don't like having that kind of relationship. It's complicated."

Orran chuckled. "I suppose it is, and dragons are simpler in a way. We don't care about what the other dragon's sex is. We fall in love with dragons without wondering what's between their legs."

Orran didn't miss the way Blake's gaze shifted to his groin. He wasn't ashamed. Now he knew he was different from Blake, and he understood why Blake was fascinated. He was, too, although he didn't have an easy task looking, since Blake was covered by clothes.

"You mean you're all pansexual?"

"I don't understand what that word means."

"It's when you like the person inside. Like, you don't care about the outside, about the body. You fall in love with the person they are."

"I think that's it, yes."

"So you could fall in love with a male dragon? You wouldn't mind that?"

Orran shook his head. "Of course not."

"What about humans? Do you think you could fall in love with a human?"

That was the question, wasn't it? Orran was pretty sure he was already falling in love with a human, but could he say it out loud? He didn't want to ignore that possibility, not when Blake was asking. He also wasn't sure he could give Blake hope, though. He didn't know what would happen to Blake once they got to the palace. The queen might have agreed to have him stay with them, but would it only be for a few days or for a longer time? Could they actually have something?

Orran cleared his throat. "I don't see why not."

"Maybe because dragons hate humans? And I actually agree with that. Most humans are dicks."

Orran barked out a laugh. "You aren't wrong. The only humans I've met before you were bad people. But you're not. I suppose that if that hypothetical human man was like you, I could fall in love with him."

That seemed to satisfy Blake, at least for now. He twisted the conversation, asking, "What's going to happen to me once we get to the palace?"

"I'm not sure. You're helping, but you're still human."

"What do you think? Will your people eventually get used to me? Can they accept me?"

Blake had said he had nothing to go back to, but Orran hadn't realized he was planning to stay at the palace. "I don't understand how you can want to stay with us," he admitted. "I know you said you don't have a family or a job, but we're dragons. Most of us won't like having you there. They'll be antagonistic, and they'll tell you to your face that they don't want you there." That wasn't a life that would be worth living.

Blake shrugged. "I don't care. I'm used to it. People are always assholes to me, except for my brother."

"Don't you want to go back to him?"

"I might if he asked me, but he won't, even though he's the only one who kept in touch with me after my family kicked me out. We text regularly, but we don't see each other often."

"You miss him." It was evident.

Blake nodded. "I do. I never told him that, mostly because I know it wouldn't change anything. He has his own life. He was good enough to reach out to me and keep in contact with me, and that's enough."

Orran could tell it wasn't. He wanted to drag Blake closer, to hug him and tell him that he was lovable, that his family should have counted themselves lucky to have him. Instead, he stayed where he was.

No human had ever lived at the palace or knew where it was or that it was there. The only humans who had ever come in were the ones who had stolen the egg, and they'd done so because they'd had inside help. Blake was different, though. "I can't make promises," Orran said. "The queen said you could come back with us, but I don't know if she'll let you stay."

"What would you do if you were in her place?"

"I trust you," Orran blurted out before he could think better of it.

Blake blinked. "You do?"

Orran realized how incredible that sounded. They'd only known each other two days, yet there he was, trusting a human. He couldn't change his feelings, though. He prayed he wouldn't be shown he was wrong, but he *did* trust Blake. "You could have stolen the baby away or hurt both of us several times. You had more than one occasion, but you're still here, and you're taking care of Blue. You're talking to me as if you see me as equal. You don't look at me like an animal. You don't look at *Blue* like an animal, even though he hasn't taken human form. So yes. I trust you."

Blake's smile was blinding. "Thank you."

"You have nothing to thank me for."

"But I do. I know you won't be the one making this decision. The queen will. But from what I understand, she trusts you."

"She does."

"Then I hope she'll trust you on this, too." Blake frowned. "Of course, you could still tell her that you don't want me there. You can tell her I shouldn't be there."

Orran wasn't going to. He might not understand why he felt the way he felt, but he was starting to fall in love with Blake, and if they continued spending time together, that would only get deeper.

To Orran's surprise, it didn't seem like such a bad thing.

"I'll tell her what I think," Orran said. "I'll explain that I trust you and that I want you to stay. I'll tell her that Blue loves you, much more than he loves me. It might take her some time to wrap her mind around everything and to make a decision, but I promise you, I'm on your side."

"I have a hard time believing that, but thank you."

Orran had a hard time believing it, too. It was what it was, though, and he wasn't going to fight his feelings for Blake. He didn't know what would happen between them, but he did know that he more than liked Blake. He wanted to see what the future held for them, but for that to happen, Blake had to be allowed to stay at the palace.

CHAPTER EIGHT

When Blake jerked awake a few nights later, he wasn't sure what had woken him. He was snuggled against Orran, with Orran pressed against his back while Blue was nestled against his chest.

It was dark because of Orran's wing draped over Blake, and he couldn't see anything. He was pretty sure he'd been having a nightmare, but just in case, he closed his eyes and breathed in and out, trying to slow his racing heart.

Then, he heard it again.

A branch cracked in the forest, and while it could have been an animal, Blake wasn't going to risk it. He couldn't, not when he had Blue with him.

Suddenly, Orran shifted. One second, Blake had a dragon at his back. The next, he had a warm human wrapped around him. Orran pressed his face against Blake's neck, and Blake couldn't help the shiver that ran through him. "Someone is here," Orran murmured.

Blake nodded. "I know."

What now, though? They had no idea who was there or how many people were there. It was probably humans, the same ones who were coming after Blake and Blue. Blake hoped his boss wasn't one of them, but he couldn't be sure.

"You need to take Blue and run," Orran said.

Blake's first instinct was to refuse. He couldn't abandon Orran. He took a moment to think before saying no, though, and he realized that Orran was right. Even if there were several humans, Orran would probably be okay. On the other hand, if Blake tried to fight and came eye to eye with a gun, he would be dead, and no one would be there for Blue.

No matter how much he hated it, he had to obey.

He nodded curtly. "I'll take care of him," he promised.

"Take him. Hide in the forest. I'll do my best to kill those humans, but I can't be sure I'll win. If I don't, if something happens to me, you need to head north. That's where the palace is. Eventually, someone will find you."

The thought of finishing this on his own made Blake want to cry. "You'll be fine," he said.

Orran chuckled softly. "I like to think so, yes. But do you really want to risk it? Do you want to risk Blue?"

They couldn't. Blake knew this might be his last moments with Orran, and he didn't know what to do about it. There wasn't time, and if Orran didn't make it, Blake didn't want him to be distracted by whatever happened now. So instead of turning around and kissing Orran, instead of telling him he was falling in love with him, he kept his mouth shut and focused on Blue.

Orran untangled their bodies and rose to his feet. He offered Blake his hand, and Blake took it, rising with the baby in his arm. Blue was blinking awake, but Blake hoped he wouldn't make any noise. He raised the baby until he could look him in the eye, then pressed a finger to his lips. "No noise, understood?" he asked.

Blue blinked again, but he nodded, and Blake hoped everything would be okay. Maybe for him and Blue, but what about Orran? There was no way for Blake to know, and he knew obsessing over it wouldn't help. If anything, it would make things even harder. He had to focus on Blue and allow Orran to do the rest.

So that was what he did. He gave Orran one last glance, then headed between the trees, in the opposite direction from where the sounds were coming from. Orran placed himself in the path of the humans who were about to stumble onto them, then shifted. He was a sight for sore eyes, even in the middle of the night, and Blake took a second to admire him. Then he turned around and fled.

They hadn't had the time to talk, and he regretted it. He wished he could have told Orran about his feelings, even if Orran would have rejected him. He wanted to come back and help Orran, make sure that he would be okay and safe. He couldn't do any of those things, though. Right now, he needed to focus on his own safety, and more importantly, on Blue's.

He stumbled, catching himself on a tree. Where could he hide the baby? He could try running away, but the humans after them would probably catch up if they managed to get around Orran. No matter how much Blake wanted to trust that Orran would kill all of them and come out of this victorious, he couldn't be sure of it. He needed to find a hiding place rather than running. Maybe if he did, if he could stash the baby somewhere and go back to help Orran.

It wasn't his job. His job was to keep Blue safe. But as long as Blue stayed where he was, it shouldn't be a problem, not as much as losing Orran would be.

Blake stopped and hesitated, biting his lower lip until he drew blood. He needed to do something. He needed to make a decision, and it was the hardest thing he'd ever done. He wanted to go back, but Orran had been clear. He had to take care of Blue first.

So that was what he was going to do. He looked around again, trying to find a good hiding place, but he realized he had a perfect one only when he looked up.

He peered at Blue. "If I climb up into one of the trees, can you stay hidden in the branches?" he asked.

Blue's eyes were wide. Blake didn't know how much he understood, but he hoped that he would get the baby to stay hidden and quiet.

Blake swallowed. "I want to go back. Orran needs me. He needs my help, and I can't let him die while protecting us. Do you understand that?"

The baby shook his head, then nodded. Blake had no idea what it meant. Still, this was the best outcome for all of them, at least for now.

"I'm going to climb up this tree," he declared. He hoped he wasn't going to fall on his face. "I'll put you down as high as I can. That way, the humans won't be able to see you from the bottom. You need to be still and quiet, though. I don't know if they'll come this way. But just in case, you can't come out until you see Orran or me. Got it?"

The baby nodded, and Blake hoped he truly had understood. He couldn't stop to check, though. He needed to help Orran, so he started climbing the tree.

It was harder than he expected. He couldn't remember the last time he'd climbed a tree. Hell, there weren't that many trees in the city. But he made do, even though his hands got scraped against the trunk and sap stuck to his skin and made him sticky and fragrant.

Once he got as high as he dared, he gently unhooked Blue from his chest, then put him on one of the branches close to the trunk. "You have to stay here. Please." The baby keened and tried to get to Blake again, but Blake shook his head. "I have to help Orran. Do you understand? I promise I'll be back." Blake hoped he would be able to keep that promise. Blue was only a baby, and it was too easy to imagine what would happen to him if neither Blake nor Orran came back.

Blake cleared his throat, hoping his emotion and fear didn't leak through in his voice. "I'm just going to see what's happening, okay? I'm going to do everything I can to help Orran, but if I can't, I'll come back and focus on you. I promise."

The baby looked terrified, and Blake hated that. He wasn't the reason Blue was afraid, though. He couldn't run away with Blue. Eventually, the humans would get to them, and everything would be worse. He truly thought their best hope was to hide, but he prayed he wasn't making a mistake. "I'll be back as soon as I can," he repeated.

The baby looked like he didn't want Blake to go, and honestly, Blake didn't want to leave. He was terrified. He didn't have a weapon, and he knew his boss. He wasn't a good person, and his men wouldn't hesitate to kill him or Orran to get to the baby.

That was why Blake needed to go.

He kissed the top of the baby's head, then started climbing down. He almost fell on his face a few times, and he heard the baby cry out in anguish. Every single time, he looked up and forced himself to smile, then pressed a finger to his lips.

He'd never been more grateful than when his feet touched the ground. He took a moment, leaning against the trunk, his knees trembling. Then, he looked up one last time. "I'm going," he murmured, hoping Blue could hear him. "I'll be back as soon as I can." And hopefully, he would have Orran with him.

Orran waited until he couldn't hear Blake and Blue anymore. Then, he opened his mouth and breathed fire on the humans coming toward them. He grinned savagely at their screams, but he knew it wasn't over by a long shot. He was surprised the humans hadn't realized that he would burn them to death. They'd probably thought they'd be able to catch him unaware, sleeping.

They'd been wrong.

Orran had woken up, and he wasn't going to stop until he was sure that all the humans were dead. He needed to protect Blue and Blake, and he was going to do it even if it was the last thing he did.

He breathed in, then breathed fire again. The trees around him went up in flames, illuminating the night. It made it easier to see the humans coming, and his heart sank. There weren't just a few of them. He didn't have the time to count, but if he had to take a wild guess, there were at least twenty, and that was without counting the dead ones. He didn't know how they'd managed to find him, especially with so many of them tramping around the forest, but they had, and now, he had to deal with them.

He breathed fire again, and while it worked at keeping some of the humans away, more reached him.

Orran prepared himself for the battle.

Luckily for him, only a few humans had guns, and those who did couldn't shoot at him. They were too close to each other, and they might shoot one of their men accidentally. Orran took advantage of that, knocking them off their feet with his wings and tail, stomping all over them once they were on the ground. They were too close by for him to breathe fire on them now, and while that was his best weapon, it was far from being the only one.

Fighting had been his life before Blue and Blake, and he knew what he was doing. He'd been trained to do this, although usually, he had help.

He reached out with his mind, hoping to get Morven's attention, but his friend was probably sleeping. He didn't answer, and Orran couldn't try for much longer because he had to focus on the fight.

He was alone. No one would come to his rescue. He was probably going to die, and there was nothing he could do about it. He *could* make sure Blake and Blue had as much time as possible to run, though, so he focused on that. He twisted his tail, knocking humans to the ground, then stomping on them with his feet. He breathed short spurts of fire, burning a few humans to a crisp. They kept coming, though, and he didn't know *where* they were coming from. How had they managed to get so many people into the forest at once? It was impossible. Or had they been following Orran since he'd left the city? Why hadn't they struck sooner, though? Maybe it was because Orran had slowly been moving toward the palace, and they were afraid they wouldn't be able to get to Blue anymore if he reached it. Whatever the reason, there were too many of them, and they were swarming Orran. He might be a dragon, bigger and stronger than them, capable of breathing fire, but he was still vulnerable.

A blade sliced into his front leg, and he screamed. The roar echoed in the forest, scaring birds from their trees.

He felt the shift coming on to him, and he couldn't do anything to stop it. He didn't know why he was shifting, but it wasn't intentional. It was a mix of pain, shock, and fear. Orran might be used to this, but that didn't mean he wasn't afraid.

He was. He was *terrified*, and he knew the end had come for him. At least he would die knowing that he'd done everything he could to get Blue to safety. He would die knowing Blake was safe, too. He wished he and the human had had time to find out where things could go between them, but he wouldn't have the chance.

He fell to the ground. His body stopped shifting, and he sat there, holding himself up on his uninjured arm, looking at the human who had hurt him. The man was still holding his knife, and his eyes are gone wide.

"Holy shit," he said. "Guys! He's human."

That was a secret Orran wished he hadn't revealed. The pain was too much for him to cling to his dragon form, though. He wasn't sure why. Usually, dragons stayed in their dragon form when they were wounded. They stayed in their dragon form most of the time.

But spending so much time with Blake had changed Orran. Orran was more in touch with his human side now. He hadn't realized it would be a bad thing, and it was too late to change it.

The humans who were left gathered around him. There were only three of them, and they were all wounded. It gave Orran a savage satisfaction. He had been the one to kill the others. Even if these guys managed to catch up to Blake and Blue, Orran was sure Blake would be able to defend the baby. One of the men looked like he might faint at any moment, and he was leaning against a tree. Another one was dragging one of his legs. The only one in decent shape was the one who'd wounded Orran, and he was still standing there, his knife dripping with Orran's blood.

Orran sat up. He wanted to get to his feet, to face death when it came, but he couldn't. His knees buckled, and he fell back to his knees.

"What do we do with him?" one of the other men asked.

The one holding the knife shrugged. "I don't know. The boss didn't say anything about dragons being able to become human. He said to bring him the baby and kill whoever tried to stop him." He looked around. "Find the baby. It has to be around here." He turned his attention back to Orran. "Can all dragons turn into humans?"

Orran pressed his lips together. He wasn't about to answer that or any other question.

The man grabbed Orran's hair and pulled. It hurt, but Orran had been through worse. He stared at the man, silently daring him to kill him. He probably would eventually, but he would try to get answers out of him first.

"Answer me," the man said, shaking Orran. "Are you the only dragon who can do this, or can the others?"

Orran kept his mouth shut. The man huffed and back-handed him, sending him to the ground. His head hit the earth, and it *hurt*. But it was nothing next to the pain in his arm. He cradled the limb to his chest, wondering what was next. Would the man torture him? Would he try to get answers out of Orran through pain? It wouldn't surprise Orran.

"We can't find the baby," one of the other men yelled.

The man holding the knife turned toward them. "Look better. It has to be around here somewhere." He paused. "Look for a human baby, too. You never know."

Orran grinned. Even though he'd revealed their secret to these humans, the humans didn't know all of it. They didn't know how shifting worked. They didn't know Blue was still a dragon, and that he wasn't alone. They probably thought Orran had killed Blake as soon as they'd left the city, and that was more than okay with Orran. They wouldn't suspect Blue was protected.

"You're not going to answer any of my questions, are you?" the man asked.

Orran spat on the ground next to the man's feet. He hoped his answer was clear.

The man shook his head. "Fine. Since you won't tell me where the baby is or how you can do that stuff, I'll kill you. Is that what you want? I'll slit your throat and harvest your body. Maybe it's worth something even though you're not a dragon right now."

Orran just stared. He saw the moment the man raised his knife. Having his throat slit would be agony, but it would be better than being tortured. Orran's instinct was to close his eyes, but instead, he looked at the man, wanting him to see who he was killing.

He regretted not giving Blake a chance. He regretted not telling the human how he felt about him. He regretted that they hadn't had more time.

The man dropped the knife. It clattered on the ground as the man opened his mouth and croaked, blood dripping from his lips.

Orran blinked at him, wondering what had happened.

Blake had arrived just in time, and his heart was still racing at the possibility of what could have happened. He'd seen that man with the knife ready to kill Orran, and he'd acted on instinct, grabbing one of the weapons from the ground and burying it into the man's back.

The man stumbled and reached out, then fell to the ground. Blake looked around, wanting to make sure that no one else was there, and he noticed two men walking around. One of them had noticed him, and he was looking at him, eyes overly bright and chin trembling.

Blake took a step toward him, and the man turned around and ran. The way he stumbled almost made Blake laugh, but he couldn't, not when Orran was still in danger and bleeding out on the ground.

There was a second man, too, and Blake brandished his weapon. It was a big knife, and he knew how much damage he could do to the guy. "Leave. I won't come after you."

The man looked from Blake to Orran. Blake didn't know why Orran had shifted, but Orran wouldn't want humans to find out about this. He should probably kill this guy, but he didn't have it in him. He might have killed the man who was threatening Orran, but it wasn't the same thing. If things came to it, he was sure other dragons could go after these guys and take care of them. They were in bad shape, and he doubted they would get very far, even if they could call for help—and Blake doubted they could, not this deep in the forest.

The man seemed to make a decision. He dragged himself back, raising his hands. He never gave Blake his back, at least not until he was far enough away to turn around and try to run. Blake waited, wondering if he was going to come back. When he didn't, he turned his attention to Orran, who was struggling to get to his feet. Blake dropped the weapon and moved toward him, helping him. "You're hurt," he said.

"What are you doing here?" Orran asked. Pain tinged his tone, and Blake knew he was pushing through it.

"I wanted to help you. I couldn't leave you alone to face them." And from the look of it, he'd been right. Not only had Orran been wounded, but with the number of dead men on the ground, Blake knew he'd fought hard. He shouldn't have left, but it was too late for those regrets.

Orran's arm was pouring blood. Blake had no idea what to do with it, but from the movies he'd watched in the past, he thought he needed to keep applying pressure on the wound. He looked around, unsure what to use, then decided it didn't matter. He grabbed one of the dead men's jackets—not one of the burned ones—and tugged it off the body. Then he wrapped the fabric around Orran's arm. It wouldn't work miracles, but it was better than nothing. "We need to get you to a hospital. To the palace. I don't know." How did those things work for dragons?

Orran shook his head. "You're going to have to take care of the wound yourself," he said through gritted teeth. "Where's Blue?"

The thought of stitching the wound was terrifying, but Blake suspected Orran was right. "I left him in a tree. Don't worry. He's safe."

"How can you know that? You need to go get him. Please."

Blake hesitated. He didn't want to leave Orran alone, even though all the humans were either dead or gone. He didn't want to risk it. He also didn't want to risk Blue, though, and he knew Orran wouldn't rest until he knew the baby was okay. "Come on," he said. He hooked an arm around Orran's waist, then dragged him ahead. "I need to get you to safety before I get the baby."

"You need to focus on him. It's your job."

"And I will. He's okay. He's going to stay in his tree until he sees me. I promise you that." Because no matter how play-ful the baby was, when he needed to listen, he did. Blake didn't know if it was instinct or because he saw him as a pa-rental figure, and right now, he didn't care.

He dragged Orran away from the carnage and the fires that were still burning around them. They went back to the spot where they'd spent the night, and he helped Orran sit against a tree.

Once Orran was settled, Blake lifted the jacket he was still holding against Orran's arm and winced. That had to hurt like a bitch, but at least the blood flow had slowed down. He placed the jacket back, then looked at Orran. "Will you be okay for a while?"

Orran nodded curtly. "I will. Go get Blue."

"As soon as I come back with him, I'll take care of your arm." He hesitated. "Please. Don't make me find you dead when I come back. I don't think I could deal with that right now."

To Blake's surprise, Orran chuckled. It jostled his arm, and he immediately grimaced , but he was still smiling. "I can't make that kind of promise, but I don't think this wound is going to kill me. Get the baby. I'll be here when you come back, and I'll be breathing."

Blake hoped that was the truth. He didn't want to go, but he realized he had to.

Leaving Orran behind was hard. Blake was more than fall-ing in love with Orran, and he hadn't realized it until now. He was already in love with him, and he didn't want to lose him before they had a chance at something. He didn't know if Or-ran would see things the way he did—if their relationship would be forbidden because of who they were, but he didn't care. He'd almost lost Orran, and he still might. He was going to do everything he could to make sure they were together, even if it meant moving to the palace and staying there forever.

When he got under the tree in which he'd left Blue, he was thankful that he hadn't too gone far. He'd left a piece of his torn t-shirt on one of the branches, so he knew he was in the right place. He looked up, but he couldn't see anything. He cleared his throat. "Blue? It's me. You can come down."

There was a rustling, then the baby's head appeared. He'd climbed lower than where Blake had left him, and Blake glared at him, then opened his arms. "You're not in trouble," he said. "I just need you to come down because we have to get to Orran. He's hurt."

Blue's eyes widened, and he scrambled down the tree so fast that he fell. He was lucky Blake was standing under it, and he caught him, pressing him against his chest and kissing the top of his head.

It was strange. Blue was not human right now, but his skin was warm, even though it was scaly. He smelled in a way that Blake had started associating with dragons, but also different. It was sweeter, gentler, the smell of a baby dragon.

Blake took a second to breathe it in and out, holding Blue against him. He couldn't waste time, though. Once he had his breathing and his heart under control again, he gently moved Blue away from his chest. "We're going back. You're probably going to be afraid, but Orran killed all the humans. Don't look around. I don't want you to see them." He wished he could avoid telling Blue all of this, but he realized it was better for the baby if he knew what they were going to find. He might not understand, but Blake needed to try. "Orran is bleeding a lot. I'm going to do everything I can to stop the blood, but I don't know if I can do anything. I'm going to need you to be a good boy, all right?"

Blue whimpered, then pressed his face against Blake's neck. Blake doubted he would get a better response, so he headed back to where he'd left Orran, praying the dragon would still be breathing when he got there.

He was.

Blake breathed easier. He put Blue down, hoping the baby would distract himself with something, but instead, he surprised Blake by crawling into Orran's lap. He curled there, keeping an eye on what was happening, not looking one bit afraid. Blake wished he could share that emotion, but he was still terrified.

He sucked in a breath and crouched next to Orran, as ready as he would ever be to clean the wound, but he realized he would need supplies — supplies he didn't have.

He got back to his feet and looked around. The humans had to have things with them. They were a long way from the city, so Blake expected to find food, clothes, hopefully, medical supplies. He walked around quickly, poking in the bushes, and found several backpacks. He dragged all of them back, and he was relieved to find something to clean the wound, what he needed to stitch it, and bandages. He tried to be quick but neat, and when he was done, he leaned back on the balls of his feet.

He was exhausted. Orran had fainted or fallen asleep when he'd started cleaning the wound, and Blue seemed to be asleep. That meant Blake couldn't allow himself to fall asleep. He needed to keep an eye on them, but more importantly, he needed to make sure the humans who had left wouldn't find them.

They had to move. He would have to carry both Orran and Blue, and he wasn't looking forward to it. If he was lucky, Orran would wake up, but he doubted it. He was too tired and in too much pain. But Blake could do this. Orran had until now, and now, it was his turn.

This time, it was Blake's job to protect the people he cared for, and he would do just that.

CHAPTER NINE

When Orran woke up, the only thing he could feel was pain. He groaned and tried to decide what *didn't* hurt him, but he couldn't. Every single movement made pain shoot through his body, his arm especially.

Then he remembered why. His eyes flew open, and he tried to get to his feet, but the pain made it impossible. A hand pressed against his chest and pushed him back, and Orran fought against it. He couldn't allow himself to be vulnerable.

"Stay still. You're going to bust the stitches," a voice said, and Orran recognized Blake. He blinked his eyes open, and he'd never been so relieved and happy to see a human. He reached out. Blake's eyes widened, but he still took Orran's hand and linked their fingers together, squeezing lightly. Then he smiled, and Orran finally allowed himself to relax. Blake wouldn't be smiling if something was wrong.

"What happened?" he asked, his voice a croak.

Blake sat next to him, crossing his legs. "You slept through the night. I checked you for fever, and you don't seem to have one, but of course, I'm no expert on dragon anatomy and illnesses. How are you feeling?"

"Like shit."

"I bet." Blake chuckled. "But you'll live, at least for a while. I worry about infections, though. I cleaned the wound as well as I could, but we should probably contact the palace and have someone who actually knows what they're doing look at you."

He was right. Dragons didn't usually get infections, but he

wouldn't put it past the humans to put something on the blade. He couldn't risk it. He looked around, relieved when he saw Blue was only a few meters away, trying to catch a butterfly. "How is he?" he asked.

"He's fine, at least physically. He seems to be okay mentally, too, but I can't tell. He was waiting in the tree when I got back to him yesterday, and he fell asleep in your lap as soon as we got here. It wasn't easy to move both of you, but I didn't want to stay where we were, just in case."

Orran turned his attention back to Blake and only now noticed how tired Blake looked. "Did you sleep last night?"

Blake shrugged one shoulder. "A bit. I didn't want to risk it. Two of the humans escaped yesterday. You should probably shift and contact the palace to tell them about this."

He was right. They had to know two humans had found out dragons could become humans, and they had to find and kill them. The secret couldn't get out. Orran would never forgive himself if it did.

He rubbed his face. "I'll shift as soon as I can," he said.

When he dropped his hand and opened his eyes, he was stunned to see that Blue had come closer. He was staring at him, his head cocked, and when Orran nodded, he climbed into his lap. It was the first time he'd done something like that. He'd warmed up to Orran, but he'd never been cuddly with him. That was reserved for Blake, and while Orran didn't understand it, he'd stopped trying. Seeing Blue act like this with him made his heart race in the best of ways.

He reached out and gently rubbed the top of Blue's head. Blue closed his eyes and leaned closer. He made a rumbling sound that caused Orran to chuckle. Blue was happy and felt safe.

Blake smiled at him. "I think he was worried about you. He's been keeping an eye on you since he woke up, although he does get distracted sometimes."

"That's normal. He's a baby."

Blake rolled his eyes. "I know that." He looked around. "So, as I mentioned, I had to move you."

Orran frowned and looked around, too. He hadn't realized it, not even when Blake had mentioned it, but he didn't recognize this place. It wasn't where he'd fought the humans, and it wasn't where he'd fainted, either. "How?"

"Well, it wasn't easy. You were out like a light, and I had to half drag and half carry you."

"How did you manage?" Orran was heavy. There was no way Blake could have done this in normal circumstances. It didn't even make sense that he had managed in *these* circumstances.

"I'm fine," Blake said. "Tired, but that's not a problem. I'm more worried about you. I also don't like the thought of staying here for much longer. I don't know if those two guys are going to look for us, but just in case, we should move."

"I agree." Orran wasn't looking forward to shifting. It normally wouldn't hurt, but he had no clue in this case. He gestured at Blue. "Why don't you take him? I'll shift, make sure he's okay, and contact the queen."

Blake nodded and reached for the baby. Blue went eagerly in his arms, and that made Orran smile. No matter how worried Blue was for him, he was still half in love with Blake.

Orran was right. It hurt when he shifted, his arm pulling, pain shooting along the limb. He focused on what he was doing, and he felt surprisingly better once he was in his dragon form. He didn't think he'd be able to walk or get into the air, though. His arm was too painful, and he didn't want to worsen the injury. He had no idea how bad it was, but from what he'd heard, he knew it would be better for him if he didn't try to move too much.

He quickly checked in on Blue, who was focused on Blake and barely looked at him. Once that was done, he focused on contacting the queen.

Your Majesty? he called out.

He held his breath, hoping the queen would answer. To his relief, she did.

Orran?

Orran briefly closed his eyes. *Your Majesty. We were attacked last night.*

There was a pause, then she asked, *The baby?*

He's fine. Blake protected him while I took care of the humans. We have several problems, though.

Tell me.

I killed most of the humans, but two of them escaped. They saw me shift to my human form. They have to be caught and killed.

I'll send a team. Where are you?

Close to the palace. Even though Blake had moved them, Orran recognized the place. *I can't fly. I was hurt last night.*

Hurt? How are you?

Blake took care of me, too. He kept the baby safe and cleaned my wound. He's afraid of infection, though, and I share that fear. I can't fly, and I can't walk as a dragon. It's too painful. I'm going to have to shift back to my human form.

I'll send two teams, one after the humans, one to get you.

Can we come home? Have you found the traitor? She hesitated, and that was enough. *Don't send anyone to get us. We'll come back on our own.*

You just said you couldn't fly, she pointed out.

I don't know. I haven't tried. But he was going to.

Try, then. I'm waiting.

Orran could hear the dare in the queen's voice. They both knew she was right and that he wouldn't be able to fly. Still, he had to try.

He extended his wings. They weren't hurt, but they weren't the important part, not when it came to the take-off. He looked around. There wasn't much space, but he would make do. He sucked in a breath, then took a step forward.

His leg buckled, and he fell to his knees.

The queen could tell what had happened before Orran told her about it. *You can't, can you?*

I'm sorry, Your Majesty.

Don't be sorry. It wasn't your fault. You were hurt protecting my son. I need one more day. Hopefully, it will be enough to catch the traitor. I'll send a team to you as soon as I can.

Orran wanted to say no. He was proud, and he wanted to finish this on his own. He knew he couldn't, though. *We'll be here.* He doubted he would be able to move even if he wanted to, and he wanted nothing less right now, not with the pain making his arm feel numb.

Soon, then, the queen agreed.

Blake should have known Orran would be stubborn. It wasn't unexpected. Orran had been stubborn since they'd met, and that hadn't changed because he'd been wounded. "Are you sure you can walk?" Blake asked him. Blake understood why asking that might make things worse, but he needed to know.

Orran scowled at him. "My arm is wounded, not my leg."

"Maybe, but you lost a lot of blood, and I'm sure you're in pain." There hadn't been any painkillers in the backpacks Blake had found. Besides, Blake didn't think he would have used them on Orran. He had no way to know how dragons reacted to human medicine.

"I'm fine," Orran insisted even though they both knew it was a lie.

There was nothing Blake could do about it, though. He was already taking care of a baby. He couldn't distract himself and take care of Orran, not more than he already was and when Orran didn't want him to. If Orran insisted he could walk, then Blake wasn't going to stop him. "Fine. Let's go, then. But we'll stop often, and we'll stop early for tonight."

From the scowl on Orran's face, Blake knew he was about

to protest again. "We don't need to stop often," Orran said.

Blake sighed. He was stubborn himself, but this was a new level of stubbornness. "I didn't say it was for your benefit. Blue is fine physically, but he's still a bit shaken, and I don't want to push him too hard."

Orran's expression softened, and he peered at the baby, who was perched on Blake's shoulder. "Of course. I should have realized."

Blake wasn't about to tell him that Blue was okay. While he was shaken, he was also more than happy to continue their traveling. He enjoyed seeing the forest, looking at the trees and birds and butterflies. He was easily distracted, just like every baby. He might be a dragon, but he was still a kid.

Blake suspected he would have lingering problems, maybe nightmares, but so far, Blue seemed to be okay. Blake hoped things would continue that way. He wanted to do more, but what? They were stuck in the forest, and now they were on foot. It wasn't going to make things easy on any of them. Hopefully, the queen would find the traitor soon and would send someone to get them, but in the meantime, they would have to make do.

So they did. After packing everything they had — and some of the things Blake had found on the humans — they headed out. Orran was doing his best to put up a brave front and to walk normally, but Blake didn't miss the way he walked curled into himself to protect his arm. He held it against his chest, and he winced every time he stumbled over a root. Blake didn't know how to help him. He wanted to, but he knew Orran wouldn't accept that help. Besides, there wasn't much he could do. The best for them would be to stop and wait for the dragons to come get them, but even that might put them at risk. The two humans who had attacked Orran had fled, and they might return with friends. That was the last thing they needed. Blake wouldn't be able to defend their little group from humans, not when there was only one of him and there would be more of them.

They were mostly silent as they walked. Blake kept an eye on Orran, just in case, and he wasn't surprised to see that Orran pushed on. He out-stubborned Blake, and Blake didn't know whether to be in awe or angry at that.

Being in pain and wounded didn't make Orran weak. Blake wished Orran understood that, but instead, he had to watch him wave his help away every time he offered. He supposed it was better than nothing. At least Orran wasn't trying to shift and fly again. That would have been a disaster.

When they finally stopped, Orran looked like he was about to faint. He was incredibly pale his skin in stark contrast with his dark blue hair. Blake tried to talk to him again and help him, but Orran waved him away, so he did his best to focus on Blue. Once they'd eaten lunch, they moved on again.

Blake wasn't sure how long they'd been walking when he decided he had enough.

He patted the top of Blue's head, then dumped his backpack on the ground. It took a second for Orran to realize what was happening, and when he did, he turned and glared at Blake. "What are you doing?"

Blake gestured around them. "What does it look like I'm doing? Stopping for the night."

"It's still early. We can get at least another hour in."

"I don't want to. I'm tired." And he was. Even though he wasn't wounded, last night had taken a toll on him. But he wasn't thinking about himself when he'd decided to stop. He could tell Orran wasn't going to be able to go on for much longer, let alone an hour. Orran would take it badly if he pointed that out, though, so he decided to play the weak human. "I'm not a dragon. I don't have the same endurance as you have. I'm tired, especially after what happened last night. You can go on if you want, but Blue and I are staying here."

Orran scowled. "I should take the baby and continue."

"You're welcome to try. I doubt he'll react better than he did the last time you tried to take him away from me, though."

They both looked at Blue, who realized he had their attention and puffed out his chest. A wisp of smoke escaped his nostrils, and he showed Orran his teeth.

Instead of getting angry, Orran chuckled. "I see. You prefer Blake to me. I don't understand why, but that's fine." He looked around, made his way to a fallen tree trunk, and heavily sat down on it. "Fine. We can stop, but you'll be the one taking care of the fire. I don't feel like shifting right now."

Blake had no idea where to start when it came to the fire, and that showed when he tried to start it. Blue was running around, looking at the birds at a safe distance, while Blake was crouched next to the small pile of wood he'd gathered. He glared at it. "I'm not going to be able to do this," he said.

"Why not?" Orran asked from his trunk.

"Because I don't breathe fire, and humans need a little help to light fires. I don't have that stuff. It's not like I was planning to go camping."

Orran sighed.

Blake didn't say anything. Even though he was irritated, he much preferred this teasing side of Orran to having Orran in pain. He didn't want them to fight. They had to stick together, at least until this was over.

Orran got up and came to crouch next to Blake. "You truly can't light it?"

"I already would have if I could."

"Fine. I'll shift."

Blake took a step back. By now, he knew how big Orran would be once he was in his dragon form. "Will it hurt you? I mean, your arm?"

Orran cocked his head. "No. Shifting doesn't hurt."

Blake was pretty sure that was a lie, at least for the moment. It had to hurt at least a bit with the wound, but he didn't say anything about it. Orran would think he thought he was weak, and that couldn't be further from the truth.

That was one of the reasons Blake waited until Blue was asleep to check in on Orran. Orran had lit the fire, and luckily, they still had some food packed away. It wasn't much, but it had been enough for the night. It helped that Blake had found granola in the backpacks.

He checked in on Blue, who was softly snoring, then turned to look at Orran, who was sitting on the ground leaning against a tree. His eyes were half-closed, and he was staring at the fire.

Blake cleared his throat. "How are you feeling?"

Orran slowly blinked. "I'm fine."

That was a lie, and they both knew it. "Are you sure?" Blake insisted. "Is there anything I can do? Anything at all to make you feel better?"

He wasn't surprised when Orran looked away. "I told you, I'm fine."

"I know. I just wanted to check. I know you're in pain, and I wish I could do something."

Orran cocked his head again, and Blake knew he was trying to understand him. That was why he wasn't surprised when Orran asked, "Why do you even care? Why are you taking care of me the way you are?"

That was an easy question to answer. "Because we're friends. Friends help each other."

"We're friends?"

Blake wanted so much more, but he doubted this was the right moment to mention it. The circumstances were less than ideal, and he didn't want Orran to freak out even more than he already was. "Of course we're friends."

"We've only known each other for a few days."

"Maybe, but I don't think it matters. Over those few days, we went through a lot. I don't think there's anyone in the world I feel closer to than you and Blue."

Orran slowly nodded as if he were turning Blake's words over in his mind and examining them. Blake knew he probably was, so he stretched out on the ground, cuddling close to Blue, and closed his eyes to sleep. He didn't want to leave Orran alone, but he suspected the dragon needed a moment to himself.

Friends. Orran liked the sound of that, yet at the same time, he disliked it. He and Blake were friends. They'd been through a lot together, and Blake had been there for Orran when Orran had almost died. He was still there for him, taking care of him, stopping for the night, even though he probably could have gone on for a few more hours. But he'd known Orran was in pain, even though Orran had been doing his best not to show it.

It was irritating, yet it was also soothing. Orran had friends at the palace, and he knew they cared about his well-being, but that was different. *Blake* was different, and Orran wanted so much more than friendship. The problem was that he didn't know how to ask for it, or even if he should. He now knew that Blake liked men, and he was a man. Well, he was a dragon. Maybe Blake only liked humans. Maybe he didn't like Orran that way. Could Orran ask for more?

Orran didn't hesitate in the face of danger. He didn't hesitate in front of a possible loss. He couldn't, not when his life and the life of his people were in danger. This was different, though. He didn't want to lose Blake, and he hoped the queen would allow Blake to stay at the palace. Blake had made it known that he wasn't planning on going back to the human city, and that was more than okay with Orran. But did Blake want more? What would happen if Orran told him he was in love with him and Blake didn't feel the same?

He didn't know. He wanted to try. This was a different kind of danger than he usually faced, though. Besides, he wasn't sure what to do with Blake when it came to having a relationship with him. All his previous relationships had been with dragon shifters. That meant that all their physical encounters had been in their dragon form. That was what Orran knew, and he *didn't* know what to do with Blake's body. He was sure he would learn if Blake allowed him to, but it still made him hesitant.

He had no idea how to express himself. He wanted to explain how hesitant he was, what he wanted, but he didn't want to push Blake into running away. Still, he'd always been courageous. The situation shouldn't change that.

He cleared his throat. "We're friends," he repeated.

He wasn't surprised when Blake turned around to face him. He stayed where he was, stretched out on the ground, but he distanced himself from the baby, probably not to wake him. He propped his head on his elbow and looked at Orran. "We are. Are you convinced of it now?"

Orran couldn't help but smile. "I never said we *weren't* friends. I just don't understand how we got so close so fast."

"I told you. We shared something not a lot of people share. I saved your life. You saved mine. We spent several days with only each other's company. We were bound to become friends."

This was it, wasn't it? It was the moment Orran needed to make a decision. "What if I didn't want us to be friends?" he asked.

He realized he'd made a mistake when the smile dropped from Blake's face. "Well, of course, we don't have to be friends if you don't want to," Blake said.

Orran shook his head. "That's not what I meant. We are

already friends. I don't want to lose that. What I meant is, what if I wanted to be more than friends with you?"

Orran was an idiot. He should be able to explain himself better than this. He shouldn't be afraid. He didn't know what to do now, and the pain pulsing in his arm wasn't helping. It was hard to focus on anything that wasn't that, even on Blake.

Blake rolled back, then sat up. He got to his knees and moved closer to Orran, and Orran waited, wondering what was about to happen. Blake stopped in front of him, leaning over him. "What do you mean, more than friends?"

Orran didn't want to have to explain this. "I've had relationships with other dragons. We were in love. It didn't work with them, but that's what I mean. I don't know if I can have a relationship with you, though. I'm a dragon shifter, and you're human. You might not be allowed to stay at the palace, and if you're not, it means we'll have to split up. Besides, I've never had a relationship with a human. What if I hurt you? What if I do something wrong? What if—"

Blake leaned closer and kissed Orran, effectively shutting him up. Orran blinked, wondering what was going on. He knew what a kiss was. He'd seen humans kiss on TV. He wasn't quite sure what to do with his own mouth now that he was the one being kissed, though.

Blake was pressing their lips together, and Orran tried to imitate his movements. He jerked away when he felt the tip of Blake's tongue against his lips, then winced at the pain in his arm.

Blake moved back, a smile on his face. "What just happened?" he asked. "Are you okay?"

Orran shook his head, then nodded. He had no idea how he felt. "I don't know. Why did you do that?"

"Why did I kiss you? Because I wanted to. Because I've wanted to kiss you for a while, and I was convinced you didn't want it."

Orran was glad to have this answer, but he wanted to know about Blake's tongue. "Why did you touch me with your tongue?" he asked, looking away.

"Because I was kissing you."

Orran needed to be honest with Blake if they were going to do this. He realized that might send Blake running the other way, but this was who he was. If Blake couldn't deal with it, Orran wanted to know it now. "I told you I've had other relationships, and that they were all with dragon shifters like me."

Blake nodded. "I heard that."

"We mostly stayed in our dragon forms. We all usually stay in our dragon forms."

Blake blinked. "I want to ask why, but I'm not sure you have an answer. I guess it's probably more comfortable for you, especially with the mind-talking thing."

Orran was grateful they weren't going down this path yet. Blake was right. He didn't know why he mostly stayed in his dragon form. "It is. But that's not why I told you this. What I meant is that all my relationships have been in my dragon form, with other dragons. I don't know how to do this, Blake. I don't know how to kiss you. I don't know how to kiss any human."

Something passed in Blake's expression, but it was gone as fast as it had come. "You mean this was your first kiss?"

Orran nodded. "It was. Dragons don't kiss."

Blake chuckled. "I see how you couldn't kiss if you're always in your dragon form. Do you want to try again?"

Orran wanted nothing more than that. "How, though? Tell me?"

Blake bit his lower lip. "Well, what I was trying to do is something called French kissing. I don't know why it's called that, so don't ask me. But basically, it's when you and your partner touch tongues. You stroke them around and against each other, things like that."

Orran ran his tongue over his lips. He didn't understand why that was pleasurable, but he didn't miss the way Blake looked at his lips when he did so. He nodded. "All right. Let's try again."

Blake's smile grew. "I have to say, I was berating your stubbornness earlier, but now, I'm happy about it."

Orran ignored him and leaned forward. Their lips touched again, and this time, he didn't move away when Blake stroked his tongue against his lips. Instead, he opened his mouth. Blake had said they were supposed to touch each other's tongues, so he pushed his forward, wondering what was about to happen.

Blake's was slick and warm. There were no other words for it, and for some reason, it sent a thrilling sensation straight to Orran's groin. He allowed Blake to take the lead, because he had no idea what he was doing, and Blake gently slid his tongue into Orran's mouth, stroking it around.

It was strange, a sensation Orran wasn't sure he could get used to, but he wanted to. No matter how strange it was, it was also pleasurable, as the pulsing in his groin told him.

When they moved apart, Blake's cheeks were flushed. Orran suspected he looked very much the same way, and for some reason, he was proud of it. He'd done that. He'd made Blake happy. "So that was kissing," he said.

Blake nodded. "It's what humans do when they're in love. Well, that, and sex, but I don't expect anything from you."

Orran suspected that just like sex between dragons, humans didn't do it only when they loved each other, but he didn't say anything about it. No matter how much he wanted Blake, he realized this wasn't the best situation. He doubted he would be able to get aroused, not with the pulsing pain in his arm.

He leaned forward again, pressing his lips against Blake's.

"I like it," he murmured.

"Yeah?" Blake's smile was soft, and Orran wanted more of it. He wanted more of everything.

Then Blue whimpered. Both Orran and Blake looked at the baby, but he was still asleep. "Probably a nightmare," Blake murmured. He looked back at Orran, and to Orran's surprise, he cupped one of his cheeks with his hand. "I want to kiss you for much longer, but I think we should go to sleep. You're in pain, and I'm exhausted."

Orran wanted to protest, but he knew better. "All right."

"Will you stay in your human form tonight? It's not as cold as the other nights."

Orran shouldn't. He should shift, just in case they were attacked. But he wanted what Blake was offering, even though he hadn't said the words. They'd slept together, snuggled against each other, every night. Orran was usually in his dragon form, but tonight would be different.

"I won't shift, if that's okay with you."

"That's what I was saying." Blake's smile widened. "Come on. Let's go to sleep. Hopefully tomorrow, someone will come for us."

For the first time since all of this had started, Orran wasn't sure he liked that idea.

CHAPTER TEN

When Blake woke up the next morning, he was warm even though Orran hadn't shifted last night. He could see *why* he was warm.

He was stretched out on his back, with Blue nestled against his chest, but that wasn't all. Orran was stretched out next to him, with his wounded arm and one leg hooked over him. Luckily for Blake, he wasn't touching Blake's cock, because he would have found out Blake was hard if he had been. It wasn't the best position, but Blake wasn't about to move.

He had no idea what was happening with Orran, but he knew what he *wanted* to happen. He didn't think he'd ever been as surprised as he had been when Orran had quietly told him that maybe he didn't want them to be friends. He'd been hurt because he'd thought Orran was telling him that once they got the baby home, they wouldn't talk to each other again. Instead, Orran had been trying to tell him that he wanted more, and Blake had almost missed it.

But when he'd realized it, they'd kissed, and it had been glorious. Blake couldn't wait to have more kisses, more gentle touches that characterized every budding relationship. He didn't know how things would go between them, but he knew that belonging to different species wasn't going to stop him. He didn't care that Orran was a dragon shifter. He cared that Orran was Orran, and that was that.

He reached out and buried a hand in Orran's hair. He'd wanted to do that since Orran had first shifted into his human form in front of him, and he was so grateful he could now.

The strands were soft and silky around his fingers, and he played with them until he realized that Orran was awake and looking at him. Then he dropped his hand as if Orran's hair had burned him.

Orran wrinkled his nose. "You didn't have to stop. I never realized it could be so pleasurable."

"I didn't mean to wake you."

"You didn't."

He was looking at Blake expectantly, so Blake obeyed and buried his fingers into Orran's hair again. He lightly tugged on it, then gently scratched Orran's scalp. Orran half-closed his eyes, looking very much like a cat, and Blake couldn't help but smile. "So if you and your partners have always been in your dragon forms, does that mean no one has ever done this, either?"

Orran opened his eyes. "It does."

Blake thought it was a pity. Dragons had two forms, and they should enjoy both of them. From the sound of it, though, they were more comfortable in dragon form. It probably made sense, but Blake hoped his presence in Orran's life would change things. It wasn't just for him. He wanted Orran to enjoy his human half, too. Dragon shifters were dragons who could become human, but that didn't negate their duality.

"We should probably get up," Orran murmured. "We have to start walking again. We're not far from the palace."

Blake knew he was right, even though he didn't want him to be. He nodded, but instead of letting Orran go, he pulled him closer and pressed their lips together. He doubted Orran would care about his bad breath, especially since they'd been traipsing around the forest for almost a week now. They both stank, but that was okay.

Once they'd kissed, they got up. Blue grumbled a bit and tried to go back to sleep in Blake's arms. Blake wanted to let him, but he was more comfortable walking with Blue on his shoulder. That way, his hands were free if Orran needed help. He gently poked the baby dragon awake, then got him to eat breakfast. He kept an eye on Orran the entire time, and he wasn't surprised to see that Orran grimaced more often than not when he moved. He was in pain, and Blake desperately wished he could do something to help.

"I need to shift," Orran said.

Blake frowned. Orran had said it didn't hurt him to shift, and Blake believed him, at least in normal circumstances. It was anything but normal, though. "Do you really have to?"

Orran looked at him. "I do want to reach out to my team and the queen. If they answer me, we'll know more about what's going on."

Blake nodded. He didn't like it, but he couldn't forbid it. "All right. We'll wait for you, then."

Orran cocked his head, but he didn't say anything, and Blake turned his attention back to Blue. He had to poke the baby again, but once he did, Blue grumbled and rolled onto his back, exposing his stomach. Blake had played with him enough to know what he wanted. He tickled him, laughing at the smoke billowing out of his nose. So far, he hadn't burned Blake, not even accidentally, and Blake was stunned. Maybe he shouldn't be. He was learning so much about dragons, and Blue was wicked smart.

"We can go," Orran said, startling Blake.

He looked at him, still stroking Blue's stomach. "Already done?"

Orran nodded curtly. "I wasn't able to contact anyone."

"That's a pity." And Blake knew why it worried Orran. He'd wanted to find out if the traitor had been found, and so did Blake. Blake wanted dragons to come to pick them up, especially Orran. He wouldn't have a problem continuing to walk, even though he was exhausted. But Orran was wounded, and he needed someone to give him painkillers and clean his wound again before it got infected. "Shall we go, then?" he asked.

Orran nodded again. "There's nothing we can do here. I told the queen we would head to the palace on foot until she sent someone to get us, and that's what we'll do."

Blake hated it. He wanted to be able to carry Orran like he was carrying Blue, but he couldn't. He doubted Orran would have allowed it. Instead, he focused on the forest around them. He stuck close to Orran, just in case, but Orran was proud, even after what they'd told each other last night.

He wasn't sure how long they'd been walking, but he had to ask, "Have you heard anything about the traitor?" Even though no one had answered Orran's calls this morning, maybe he'd managed yesterday. Blake couldn't hear what was said, and he was curious.

Orran shook his head. "I told you. I wasn't able to contact the queen this morning."

"Do you have any idea who the traitor could be?"

Orran hesitated. "I suspect one of the queen's family members. Probably one of her cousins."

"Let me guess. They don't think she should be queen, and they want to take her place since she doesn't have an heir with the egg gone."

Orran looked surprised. "Exactly. How did you know that?"

Blake shrugged. "You guys might be dragons, but you're also human. That means I probably understand you better than you think."

Orran was thoughtful. "I suppose that's right, at least in part. You understand our instincts better than you expected because we're not animals."

Blake winced. "The only reason I thought you were animals was that I didn't know you could shift into a human being. You can't blame me for that."

"I don't. You've been respectful since the beginning. You helped me with Blue. I'm not trying to offend you, Blake. I'm just trying to understand you the way you apparently understand me."

Blake offered Orran his hand. He knew Orran was about to say no to taking it, but he wiggled his fingers and explained, "I'm not offering to take your hand because I think you can't do this on your own or that you're weak. This is another thing humans in love do. They hold hands. It makes them feel closer to each other."

Orran didn't look convinced. "Are you sure?"

"I wouldn't lie to you, Orran. I promise." Because he was pretty sure that if Orran ever found out he was lying about anything, that would be it for them. He didn't want that to happen. Honesty was hard, but when it came to this relationship, he was more than happy to work with it.

Holding hands wasn't as bad as Orran had thought it would be. Once Blake had explained why he wanted to do it, he'd understood better. It was obvious that he had a lot to learn if he wanted to be in a relationship with Blake, but he was more than willing to do that.

He wanted Blake in a way he'd never wanted anyone else. He'd loved his past partners, but Blake was different. Maybe it was because of the situation they were in, or because he was human. Orran didn't know, and he didn't think it mattered. The only thing that did matter was how he felt, and of course, how Blake felt.

Orran had thought their time together was coming to an end. Even once they got to the palace, he'd thought Blake would be too busy exploring and getting to know other dragons, but instead, Blake wanted a relationship with Orran.

Orran didn't know how it would work or whether the queen would have anything to say about it, but they wouldn't find out until they tried, and he was willing to do just that. He was ready to do a lot when it came to Blake, but now wasn't the right moment to make decisions. He was in too much pain, and he couldn't think straight.

"I think we should stop," Blake said.

Orran suspected he'd noticed he was stumbling. The pain was getting to him, even though it was in his arm and not his leg. But his arm felt like it was dead except for the pain, and he was starting to worry.

He knew some dragons who had lost a limb in battle, so he realized it wouldn't be the end of the world. It also wouldn't be easy for him, though. He would have to relearn how to take flight, how to live with one limb missing. He didn't know if he could do that. "A little bit more," he said, gritting his teeth.

Blake looked at him. "You know you don't have to impress me, right? I already know you're tough."

Orran shook his head. It wasn't for Blake's benefit, but since the queen had told him she would send someone to get them, he didn't want to be seen as weak by those dragons. They would already have something to say about the fact that he was with a human, and it would be even worse when they realized that Orran and Blake weren't just friends. Orran had no idea how they would react, and he needed to make sure they didn't see him as less than he'd been before. That meant standing on his own two feet and pushing ahead. "I know *you* don't think that. I can't risk any dragon seeing me this way, though."

Blake blinked. Then, he grimaced. "Don't tell me dragons think you're weak if you can't stomp humans to death?"

That startled a laugh out of Orran. "No. Most dragons see wounds as normal, since we often fight with dragons belonging to other clutches or with humans. Some dragons are assholes about it, though, and I can't be sure who will pick us up and when."

Blake glared. "I don't care. They shouldn't look at you as weak, because you're not. I'll be more than happy to tell them if they ask."

That touched Orran more than he'd thought anything could. Blake was willing to defend him even against dragons, and it was incredible. Orran supposed he shouldn't have been surprised, though. This was what Blake was like. "Will you stay at the palace, then?" he asked, changing the topic.

Blake's expression told Orran that he knew what was happening, but that he was going to go along with it. "If your queen allows me to, yes," he answered.

"She already said you could."

"She did. I'm happy about that, but has she mentioned how long she'll allow me to stay?"

She hadn't. Orran knew that was because she didn't know Blake and she wasn't sure what to think about the fact that her son had clung to a human, but he hoped that once she got to know him and she realized he was a good man, she would allow him to stick around. "What if she says you can stay? What will you do?" Because one of Orran's fears was to lose Blake to the human world. It was one of the reasons he wasn't sure what to do. He wanted to be with Blake. He couldn't deny that, not anymore. But was he going to lose Blake to the humans?

Blake took his time answering, probably because he knew how important the question was. "I can't promise you I won't ever go back to the city," he began. Orran's heart squeezed, but he forced himself to listen. "I mean, there's my brother. We might not be close, but I still love him. But for the rest, I truly am not planning to go back. There's nothing waiting for me there. No one. If I can find a family with you and other dragons, then I want that to happen."

Orran's heart felt like it swelled. "You'll always have a family with me, even if you leave," he promised.

Blake looked at him, his cheeks reddened. "Really?"

Orran nodded. "I know we're very different, but I don't think it means we shouldn't be together. I realize it won't be easy, especially when we have to face other dragons. Some of them will have something to say against your presence there. They will be vocal about it. Some might even try to attack you."

Blake's eyes widened. "Will some of them try to burn me to a crisp?"

"I don't know. We have no way of knowing until we get there. Some won't be happy about the queen allowing you to stay, though. I know that for sure. They might even try to point it out as a reason the queen shouldn't be in charge anymore." Which was why she might not allow him to stay longer than absolutely necessary.

Blake grimaced. "I don't want to cause trouble to anyone, least of all her and you. Maybe I should go back,"

Orran shook his head and squeezed Blake's hand. "I don't want you to go back. We don't know what will happen, but you're mine. Even if some of the dragons have something to say about that and will think I'm crazy, I don't care. It doesn't change how I feel about you."

Blake's smile was hesitant. "So you're going to claim me as yours in front of them?"

"I will. I wasn't planning on keeping you a secret. If we decide to do this, whatever *this* is, I won't hide it. I'm not ashamed of being with you, Blake." How could he be? Blake was a good man, even though he wasn't a dragon shifter. People would realize that if they gave him a chance, just like Orran had. The problem was that he didn't know if they would. He hoped so, but he couldn't force anyone.

"I don't want you to have to choose between your life and

family, and me," Blake murmured. "It wouldn't be fair."

"But you wouldn't be the one asking me to choose, would you?"

"I would never do that."

Orran leaned forward, ignoring the pain in his arm, and kissed Blake's cheek. "See? You care about me."

"I do."

"That's more than some people in the palace can say. It's like a small city, Blake. Not everyone knows each other, and not everyone *likes* each other. But that's fine. As long as the people I love are okay with this, I'll be okay. I don't care what others think."

"I hope that's the truth. But more than that, I'm scared that you'll have to choose between staying at the palace and coming with me. I don't think I could forgive myself if that happened."

Orran shook his head. "We can't know what will happen. You might freak out and leave, or you might decide to stay." The first part especially terrified Orran. Blake might have seen him naked, but neither of them knew if their bodies were compatible for making love. Orran had never had to think about that, but now, he did, and he didn't know they could make this work or what Blake would think.

But no. They *could* make this work. Orran was convinced of that.

A movement in the sky caught his eye, and he looked up. "I think they're here."

Blake's eyes widened. He turned his attention to the sky. "The dragons the queen said she would send?"

"I think so." But Orran couldn't be sure. "It could be someone else. The traitor might have found out about Blue, and he might be trying to get rid of him."

"I see." To Orran's surprise, Blake let go of his hand, took Blue off his shoulder, and handed him to Orran. "Keep him safe." Then, he put himself in front of Orran as if to protect him.

Blake had no idea what was going on. He hoped the dragons landing in front of them had been sent to help him and Orran, but he couldn't be sure. What if instead of the queen, the traitor had sent them? What if that person had found out about Blue and was here to kill or kidnap the baby? Blake couldn't risk it, and even though he knew it was futile, he placed himself between Orran and the dragons. He wouldn't be able to do much, but maybe even that little he *could* do would give Orran time to escape. He could run away and hide in the forest with Blue.

"What are you doing?" Orran murmured.

Blake shook his head without looking at him. "Shut up. I'm trying to protect you."

"Protect me? You're human."

"So?" Blake hissed. "I protected you when we were attacked. I can do it again." Even though it would no doubt end with him dead. But if it meant that Orran and Blue had a chance, he was going to make sure they did. His life was worth theirs.

The dragons landed. There were three of them, and they were majestic. Blake had never seen a dragon from so close until Orran, and he hadn't realized how different they could be. Not only did their colors differ, but their features did, too, just like two people might. Their eyes were spaced and shaped differently, and the spikes on their backs were of various shapes. All of that made it easy to identify them, so Blake hoped that if he did end up living in the palace, he would be able to do that.

One of the dragons landed right in front of him, took a step back when they saw him, then reared forward. Blake almost closed his eyes. He didn't want to look death in the face.

The dragon didn't touch him, though. Orran put a hand on Blake's shoulder and pulled him back, then stepped away from him. Blake turned around, hooking an arm around Orran's waist and trying to pull him back. "You know them?" he asked.

Orran nodded. "I do. It's my team."

Blake relaxed, but not entirely. Orran and Blue were safe. He wasn't.

Blake looked at the dragon. They were a beautiful emerald green, but they didn't hold a candle to Orran. He was the most beautiful dragon Blake had ever seen, and Blake knew it wouldn't change. Of course, he suspected it was because he was in love with Orran, but still.

"Can you shift?" Orran asked.

The dragon's eyes narrowed. Blake couldn't believe he had never realized that dragons could become humans. They behaved like humans in some ways, like in the way their faces expressed their feelings. Of course, since he'd never seen a dragon from this close before meeting Orran, it would explain why he hadn't suspected.

It was obvious this dragon didn't want to shift, maybe because he didn't want their secret to be out, although it was too late, since Orran was in his human form. He took a few moments, probably to talk with the other two dragons behind him, then shifted.

The dragon looked like Orran, yet not. His hair was cut short, and it was green. He also looked angry, and Blake wasn't sure what to do about that. He realized these dragons didn't know him and probably didn't trust him the way Orran did, but he hoped they would give him a chance. He *needed* them to give him a chance. He didn't want to die here in the forest after everything that had happened, and especially not after he finally had Orran in his life. He was ready to risk just about anything to make them see they could trust him, or at the very least, that they should take him to the palace. Maybe if they gave him more time, they would understand they could trust him. Blake realized the chances of that happening were small, but they were there.

"What's going on?" the dragon asked.

Orran turned to Blake and handed Blue off to him again. The other dragon's eyes widened, and he stepped forward, but Orran moved toward him and shook his head, raising a hand to stop him. "Let them be."

"Let them be? You just handed the heir to the throne to a human."

"I know what I'm doing. The heir to the throne has been with him for more than a week. Don't worry about it."

"The queen—"

"She knows about Blake, as I'm sure you're aware."

The dragon didn't look convinced. Blake stayed right where he was, tightly hugging Blue. He didn't know what was about to happen, but if these were his last moments with the baby, he wanted to make the most of them. He murmured in Blue's ear, telling him he loved him, and he kissed the top of his head. He hoped that whatever happened, Blue wouldn't be afraid, but he knew the chances of that happening were slim. Blake had been there since Blue had come out of his egg. To have him taken away wouldn't be easy on Blue, especially not after what had happened the other night.

But if it kept Blue safe, Blake would do it. He would do just about anything for Orran and Blue, whether or not they asked.

"*What* does the queen know?" the dragon asked.

"I contacted her the other day and explained to her what had happened with Blake."

"Why didn't you tell me?"

There was pain in the dragon's voice, and it told Blake that he and Orran were close. It would make sense, since they were part of the same team, but he couldn't help but feel jealous.

He realized it was stupid. Why should he be jealous of the relationship between Orran and this dragon? They could be friends. Orran had said nothing about being in a relationship, and while dragons were different, Blake didn't think they were so different that he wouldn't mention being in love with someone else.

Or at least, he hoped they weren't. He didn't have anything against throuples, but he was in love with Orran, and he didn't want anyone else in their life, not that way.

He sucked in a breath. He couldn't think like this. He didn't know what was happening or who these dragons were. He had to give Orran the time to fix things and to explain. He needed to trust him, and he did.

He didn't trust the three new dragons, though.

"Don't worry about that. He can be trusted," Orran said.

The dragon stared at him for a moment, then nodded. He turned to Blake, and Blake waited to see what he would do. The dragon might believe Orran when Orran said he could be trusted, but Blake doubted that would be the case. The only reason Orran had started to trust him was that he'd spent time with him. This dragon hadn't.

The dragon reached for Blue. Blake could have told him what would happen if he tried to take Blue away, but the dragon was too fast, and he hooked his hands around the baby.

Blue didn't take it well. He twisted his head around and snarled, then breathed fire right in the dragon's face, who snatched his hands away. The dragon jumped back and stumbled, almost falling. He managed to catch himself on a tree, but his eyes were wide. "Why did he do that?"

Orran chuckled. "I told you Blake can be trusted. There's a

reason for that. Blue hatched when he was with him, and he loves him. More importantly, he trusts him, and Blake has done nothing to show that trust was misplaced. I tried taking him away, too, in the beginning, and he had pretty much the same reaction. After what happened the other day with humans, I don't want to take him away from someone he feels safe with."

The dragon didn't look convinced. Still, there wasn't much he could do. Eventually, he nodded. "All right. Let's head to the palace. The queen can see to this herself."

"Thank you," Orran murmured. "I would have flown home on my own, but—" He raised his arm to show the dragon he was hurt.

The dragon's expression softened, and he patted Orran's shoulder. "Don't worry about that. You were wounded protecting the heir. No one will say anything about it." He turned his attention to Blake. "I'm going to shift again. You and Orran can ride with me."

Blake was relieved he wouldn't have to ride alone, either on this dragon or one of the other two. He didn't particularly want to climb on this guy's back, but he knew he had no choice.

So that was what he did. He helped Orran settle onto the dragon's back, then sat behind him, Blue sandwiched between the two of them. He sucked in a breath, knowing that whatever happened next would change his life forever.

He didn't know what the future held, but he hoped it would have Orran and Blue in it.

CHAPTER ELEVEN

Blake almost didn't realize they had arrived at the palace. For some reason, he'd expected it to be like the ones in human fairytales—white, standing in the middle of a city, proud and obvious.

The dragons' palace was very different.

It was built into the side of a mountain. It wasn't visible from a distance, but once they got close enough, Blake noticed the openings in the stone wall. It wasn't just a mountain, either. The dragons had built on top of it, and even though the additions looked like they were part of the mountain, from up close, it was obvious they weren't natural.

Blake didn't know what to think about it, but then, no one cared what he thought about it. He kept his mouth shut as the dragon he and Orran were riding rose to the top of the mountain. He entered what looked like a crater, and Blake realized it was a landing pad. He held his breath, but the dragon didn't have a problem landing. It wasn't even jarring, which was a relief, since Orran was still in pain.

Blake was grateful to be able to climb off the dragon's back. He was still holding Blue, and the baby climbed onto his shoulder so Blake could help Orran down, too. Orran was a little paler than he'd been before, and Blake leaned closer. "Are you okay?" he murmured.

Orran nodded. "I'll be fine. It's painful, but nothing I can't stand."

Blake wasn't convinced, but he understood that Orran didn't want to show weakness to his team. Blake hated that he felt like that, but he didn't know how dragons worked when they were with each other. He didn't know what would happen if the other dragons thought Orran was weak. He also didn't want to think about it. He had enough to focus on and worry about right now.

The dragon who had carried them shifted again. He stepped closer to Orran, and Blake took the opportunity to look around.

There were dragons *everywhere*. He supposed he should have expected it, but he hadn't realized that so many dragons lived here. They were all in their dragon forms, too, and it was a sight Blake had never thought he'd see.

He didn't know what to do except stand there, but he was grateful none of the dragons tried to come close to him. Most of them were staring at him, probably not believing that a human was in the palace, but they didn't do anything, and he relaxed. He didn't know what he would have done if one of these dragons had confronted him or tried to hurt him, and he didn't want to find out.

"I'm sorry," the dragon said.

Blake turned his attention back to him. Orran looked pissed, and Blake knew that whatever happened next, it wouldn't be good for him.

"You can't do this," Orran snapped. "The queen knows about him. She agreed to have him with us."

"She's the one who asked for him to be taken away," the other dragon said.

Orran took a step back. "It can't be. She would have told me."

The other dragon looked sorry, and Blake suspected he was. He also wouldn't hesitate to step in if Blake refused to do whatever he and Orran were talking about, though. "I'm truly sorry," he repeated. "I have to follow orders, though."

Orran opened his mouth, and Blake had to intervene. He cleared his throat and stepped closer to them. Orran looked at him, and he appeared ready to grab him and fly away if that was what was needed to keep Blake safe.

But he *couldn't* fly away. They had to face this. "I'll come with you," Blake told Orran's friend.

The dragon's eyes widened. "You will?"

"Of course. I understand why none of you trust me. That trust will need to be built." That would only happen if they didn't kill him, but he couldn't think they would, not if he wanted to get through this.

He reached for Blue and gently unhooked him from his shoulder. "Here," he said, handing him over to Orran. "Take care of him." Blake smiled. "He's going to meet his mother, isn't he?"

Orran rubbed the top of Blue's head. "He is."

Blue tried to get back in Blake's arms, and it made Blake's eyes burn with tears he didn't want to shed. Orran didn't want the other dragons to see him as weak, and neither did Blake.

He leaned forward and gently kissed Blue's head. "You'll be okay," he murmured. "I'm not going anywhere. You're going to meet your mom, and I'll be right here when you come back. Okay?" He still had no idea if Blue understood him, but he needed to say it.

"I'll make sure nothing happens to you," Orran said. "I'll talk to the queen. I didn't know this would happen."

"I know."

"I would have told you otherwise."

Blake wanted to kiss Orran, just in case it was the last time he could. He didn't know how the others would react, though, so he limited himself to taking Orran's hand, then gave it a squeeze before letting go. "I *know*."

Then Blake turned toward to the other dragon. He didn't want to start crying in front of him and the others, and that was what would happen if he continued this. "Where should

I go?"

The dragon was looking at him strangely, but he gestured at the other two. They moved closer, and he never took his focus away from Blake as he ordered, "Shift. You'll take him."

One of the dragons shifted right away, but the other took a moment. When he did, he looked pissed. "Why can't we take him away in our dragon form?" he asked.

The dragon who had carried Blake and Orran looked at him. "Because I say so. The queen wants him to be comfortable."

"He's a human."

"It doesn't matter. We're not beasts. We don't kill people who helped us."

Blake had no idea what it meant that the queen wanted him to be comfortable. She was taking him away from Orran and Blue, and that meant that he wouldn't be okay until he saw them again and was sure they were fine.

Still, he went with the dragons. He didn't have a choice. Thankfully, they didn't touch him. Instead, they stepped to the side as he moved between them, and together, the three of them headed away from the landing platform. They passed through an archway in the wall, and Blake had no idea what to expect. He was tempted to give Orran and Blue one last glance, but he suspected he would cry if he did, so he kept his head high and his gaze up front.

They were in a well-illuminated hallway. It was wide enough that two dragons in their dragon forms could walk side by side. The illumination came from lamps on the walls. They looked out of place, even though the walls were polished and smooth. Orran had told Blake about the cameras that had filmed the humans who'd entered the palace, so he knew that even though the palace was in the middle of nowhere, it had modern amenities.

He'd expected dampness and cold, since they were inside

a mountain. Instead of going down, though, the dragons led him forward, then, when they reached a central round room with a well in the middle, up. Large ramps twisted upward, with an archway at every landing. The ramps ran along the walls, but there was enough space in the middle for dragons to fly up and down if they didn't want to walk.

Blake followed the two dragons escorting him toward one of the ramps. He knew he would get lost if he was left alone. Luckily for him, he wasn't. He was out of breath after only a few minutes of walking uphill. Wide windows punctuated the walls along the ramp, and Blake couldn't turn his head quickly enough to take in everything there was to see. He felt like a child on Christmas morning, and he hoped that his Christmas wasn't going to end in his death. The queen seemed not to want to kill him, at least not yet, but he wouldn't put it past someone else to try to do just that.

They finally stopped climbing. They entered another hallway, and this one, too, was well lit. The light from the lamps illuminated the painted stone walls. Blake had expected to be taken to a cell, but the only thing he could see was a row of doors, one on each side of the hallway. They might still be cells, but the hallway was too pretty to be a prison.

They kept walking, the dragon who'd protested was still grumbling until they stopped in front of one of the doors. The other one pushed the door open and stepped aside, and Blake knew he'd arrived. He sucked in a breath, then stepped into a bedroom. It was made for a dragon, so it was wide, and the windows were huge, one of them opening onto a spacious balcony.

"You'll find clean clothes in the bathroom," the dragon who'd opened the door said.

Blake realized she was probably a female from her voice and a part of her anatomy, which he'd done his best not to look at, but he wasn't about to ask. "Thank you."

She nodded. "Someone will bring you food."

"Okay," Blake said. He had no idea what else to say.

She hesitated. "You can't leave this room yet. There will be guards outside, so don't try it."

"I'm not planning on going anywhere. I know I'm a guest here, and I have to follow your rules." And this was much better than what he'd expected. He didn't like the thought of being a prisoner, but it could be worse.

Much, much worse.

She still seemed unsure, but to Blake's surprise, she smiled at him. "My name is Octavia. I'm part of the team Orran put together to look for the egg. You protected both Orran and the egg."

"I did."

"Thank you. I hope this is okay for you," she said, gesturing at the room.

"It's more than okay. Trust me." Blake looked around again as she and the other dragon stepped out. If this was a prison, it was the best jail cell he could have had. It didn't mean everything was okay in his life, but since he wasn't in a damp, dark cell, he hoped it meant that the queen would eventually release him from the bedroom and that he would see Orran and Blue again. He didn't know what would happen if he was refused that, but his heart broke just at the thought of it.

Orran was frightened. Not for himself, but for Blake. He doubted anything would happen to Blake, not when the queen knew how important he was to her son, but still. Orran hadn't expected them to be separated as soon as they reached the palace, and now he wasn't quite sure what to do.

Blue was in his arms, and he was making a keening sound that went straight to Orran's heart. Blue was trying to get out of his arms to get back to Blake. Orran held him tight, though. If the queen wanted Blake to be under arrest, that was what would happen. Orran and Blue didn't have anything to say about it, and they couldn't stop it.

"Why is he doing that?" Morven asked.

Orran glared at him, even though he knew this wasn't his fault. "What do you think? He wants to get back to Blake."

Morven's eyes widened, and he took a step back. "I'm sorry I asked."

Orran took in a deep breath. "I'm sorry I snapped. I shouldn't have. I know you have your orders and that you have to obey them."

Morven nodded. "You're right. I'll admit I don't like or trust the human, but you do, and that's enough for me. Besides, I've seen how he is both with you and the baby. I don't think he's a bad man."

"You don't?" That surprised Orran. Knowing what he did of Morven, he'd expected Morven to hate Blake on sight.

Morven shrugged. "I guess only time will tell."

"Do you know why the queen wanted him arrested?"

"We didn't arrest him. She said he had to be confined to one of the guest bedrooms, and I obeyed. I didn't ask her why. You'll have to do that yourself, if you want to find out." He gestured toward the entrance of the palace. "Ready to go?"

Orran was. He knew the queen wanted to see her son, and he didn't wish to keep Blue away from her for any longer. No matter how terrified he was for Blake, he knew nothing would happen to him. He didn't like the thought of Blake being confined, but he was safe, and he would stay safe until Orran could get to him.

Orran held Blue tighter, and as he followed Morven to the queen's rooms, he gently talked to him. "He's going to be fine," he murmured. "Your mother wants to see you, but I'm sure that she'll free Blake soon. She just wants to make sure he's safe."

Baby dragons didn't understand everything, just like human babies didn't, but Orran hoped that what he was saying was at least soothing to Blue. Blake and Orran were the only people Blue had known since he was born, so everything that was happening was bound to scare him. Hopefully, having Orran with him was helping. Orran realized that Blue didn't love him as much as he loved Blake, and while there wasn't a reason for that, he didn't doubt it. He was doing everything he could to help the baby, but he knew Blue would be anxious until he saw Blake again.

That was worrying. Blue's mother might get offended by how much her son cared for a human. It wasn't Blue's fault, just like it wasn't Blake's, but it was what it was. The two had come together in a moment of need, and it would influence their relationship for the rest of their lives. The queen might want to keep Blake away from Blue. It wouldn't be like her, but Orran didn't know how she would react when it came to her son. Blue was her first baby and the heir to the throne. He was important to her, but also their entire clan.

In short, Orran had no idea what was going to happen, or what he would do if things went the wrong way. He couldn't exactly take Blake and run, although he was tempted to do just that. Blake didn't want him to have to choose between the clan and him, and Orran didn't want that, either. He didn't want the queen to push him into it, but he was aware of what might happen.

He loved the clan. He loved his fellow dragons, and he loved the queen. They weren't friends, but she'd always been just, and he'd been more than happy to support her when she'd taken the throne. He hoped she would make the right decisions in this case, but if she didn't, maybe she wasn't the person Orran had thought. Maybe she didn't deserve his devotion.

Or maybe she did, and Orran was overly sensitive when it came to Blake. He would never have believed it if someone had told him a month ago that he would fall in love with a human, but that was what had happened, and now he had to deal with the consequences. Even though he knew Blake loved him, too, it didn't solve all their problems.

Love rarely did.

"He's been taken care of," Morven murmured as they walked along the hallways.

"He's imprisoned," Orran said, his voice too harsh.

"He is, but he's not in a cell. He's in a guest bedroom. I know you worry about him, even though I don't understand why. You need to relax, though. Nothing will happen to him. The queen doesn't trust him, but apparently, she knows what happened with him. I contacted her on our way back. She knows he took care of her son."

"I told her about it, yes." And that was the reason she'd agreed to have Blake at the palace. Orran should have realized it wouldn't be as easy as he'd thought.

"Then give it time. She probably wants to meet him, and since she doesn't know him, she won't allow him to run around the palace yet. Don't start freaking out. Everything isn't lost."

Orran didn't say it, but everything felt lost to him. Morven couldn't understand. He hadn't spent more than a week alone with Blake in the forest. He didn't know Blake the way Orran did.

He didn't know Orran was in love with Blake.

They finally reached the throne room. Orran wasn't surprised when instead of stopping there, Morven guided him toward the small room behind it. The queen would want the reunion to be in private. She would want to be able to cry, to hug her baby, and to be a mother before a queen, even if it wasn't for very long.

She was already in the room when Morven opened the door. She looked up, and her eyes widened when Orran stepped into the room. She rushed toward them, almost knocking him out with one of her wings. She froze just before she could touch Blue with her snout. Her eyes glittered, and she looked at the baby, who was still cuddled against Orran's chest. Blue wasn't moving but staring at her with even wider eyes.

To Orran's surprise, the queen shifted. "How is he?" she asked. She reached for him, but once again, she stopped before touching him.

"He's fine, at least physically," Orran told her. "He's sad because Blake was taken from him."

The queen looked away. "I apologize for that, but it needed to be done. You trust him, and I want to trust him, too, just because of that. I still have to talk to him first, though."

"I understand." And Orran truly did. She was the queen. She couldn't think only about her son, or even herself. The clan was more important, and Orran could too easily imagine what they would have done if a human had been allowed to roam the palace without explanation.

The queen opened her arms and waited for Blue to climb into them. Orran didn't know if he would, but he was only half surprised when the baby dragon finally agreed to it. He didn't know his mother, but he'd only been born a week ago. He was young, and he would come to love her.

"Thank you," the queen said, holding her son tightly to her chest.

Orran nodded at her. "It was my pleasure, Your Majesty."

She snorted softly. "You're wounded. I doubt that was a pleasure."

"The wound wasn't, but I'm still happy I did this. I'm happy to get your son back to you."

She looked at Orran. "Are you also happy you met a

human?"

She saw too much for Orran to be comfortable with, but he supposed that if Blake stuck around, she would find out about their relationship anyway. "I was. I didn't trust him in the beginning, and I was wary, but I trust him." He hesitated. "And I love him."

The queen took a step back, but to Orran's surprise, she didn't berate him for falling in love with a human. "I can't make any promises. I know I told you he could stay, and as far as I'm concerned, he can. He saved my son, and I'll always be in debt to him. We have to make sure that the clan accepts him, though. It will be too dangerous for him to be here if they don't. I'll talk to him tomorrow, and we'll take it from there."

"Thank you," Orran said as he bowed his head.

"You should see a healer and wash up. I want to spend time with my son."

"Of course, Your Majesty." He hesitated. He probably shouldn't say this, but he had to. "Blake named your son Blue."

She blinked and looked down at her baby. Blue still seemed unsettled, but he wasn't crying out, and he wasn't trying to get back into Orran's arms. "He named him?"

"Only because he didn't want to refer to him as the baby. I thought you should know."

She nodded thoughtfully. "Thank you. Now go." She looked at him and smiled. "Once you're done cleaning up, Morven can tell you in which bedroom your friend is."

That was as much of a benediction as Orran would get, and he knew it. For the moment, it was enough. He didn't know if it would still be enough in the future, but there was nothing he could do about it for now.

Blake was bored. He supposed he should consider himself

lucky that he was still alive to feel bored, and he was. He'd expected the dragons to kill him and put him into their stew when they'd taken him away, and he still wasn't convinced that wasn't going to happen. He hadn't seen Orran since they'd been separated, and even though he'd asked the guards at his bedroom door about him, they hadn't told him anything. They'd barely even looked at him, and he hadn't dared to insist. They were all in their dragon forms anyway, and he didn't fancy being a snack.

So here he was, bored, worried, and with no idea what was going to happen to him or how Orran was doing.

He paced the length of the bedroom, stopping at one of the windows to look at the forest. The palace was beautiful, and Blake felt tiny, even in the bedroom. It was meant for a dragon, with the bed that looked more like a nest than any-thing Blake was used to and enough space for an adult dragon to move without trouble. It seemed to take Blake five minutes to pace from one side of the room to the other.

All right, maybe that was an exaggeration, but not by much. The bedroom would be spacious even for a dragon, and he wasn't one, so it felt even bigger.

He moved to the nest bed and dropped onto it. It felt strange, but not uncomfortable. It was soft under him, and he knew he'd be able to sleep without a problem—that was, as long as he found out what had happened to Orran and Blue.

Blake knew Blue had to be with his mother right now. He wished he'd been there to see the reunion, but it wasn't his place. He doubted he would have been present even if he were a dragon. It was a private moment, but he hoped the queen knew how much he cared for Blue.

He huffed and moved to get back to his feet. He was too twitchy to stay still for more than a few seconds, no matter how comfortable the bed was.

Getting back up wasn't as easy as getting onto the bed,

though, not for a human. He had to roll to his knees, and of course, that was when the bedroom door opened.

Blake scrambled to get up, not wanting to be vulnerable even though he doubted the dragons would hurt him. They wouldn't have fed him, and he'd be in a jail cell. The bedroom was far from being that, even though he couldn't leave it right now.

Orran stepped in. Blake almost fell on his face in his haste to get to him. He didn't know what to call Orran — boyfriend? Partner? Both of those felt inadequate, but Blake didn't have a better word for it — and it didn't matter, not now. He rushed toward Orran but stopped right before throwing his arms around him. "Are you okay? I was getting worried," he said. He didn't want to hurt Orran by hugging him, but he also wasn't sure what Orran would want from him now that he was back where he belonged.

The forest and the time they'd spent together there felt so far away, as if it had never happened. Blake wouldn't be surprised to wake up and find out all of it had been a dream, but until that happened, he would make the most of it.

Orran smiled. "I'm fine."

Blake looked at Orran's wounded arm. It was bandaged, so he couldn't see how bad it was, but he remembered it all too well. "Shouldn't you be in your dragon form?" Blake wasn't sure it would help, but he remembered that Orran didn't usually spend a lot of time in his human form. He'd expected him to shift now that he was home.

Orran reached back and closed the door, and Blake had just the time to see one of his guards staring at them. He couldn't read the dragon, and he didn't try to. He didn't care what they thought, especially not now that Orran was with him.

"I'm fine like this," Orran said.

"Are you sure? I know you prefer your dragon form, and I don't want you to be uncomfortable because of me." It would make having a conversation hard, but Blake could deal with it.

He could deal with a lot of things if it made Orran happy.

"I'm fine, Blake. And before you ask, my arm is fine, too. It will heal without trouble. You did well, taking care of me. The healer was impressed."

Blake felt the last of the tension in his body drain away. "Thank God. I wouldn't have been able to forgive myself if you'd been permanently damaged." Blake paused, mentally berating himself. "Not that it would change how I feel about you. I still want to be with you, but I'll understand if you changed your mind. We're not alone in the forest anymore, and we have to consider everything. I mean, I don't even know if your queen will allow me to stay."

Orran cocked his head. "Do you want to stay?"

"You know I do."

"Are you still sure? You've seen the palace now. You've seen the dragons, and you've talked to some of them. You know what you'd be going against if you don't change your mind."

Blake stepped closer. He desperately wanted to touch Orran, but this conversation felt too important to get distracted. "I haven't changed my mind." Blake hesitated. He didn't know how Orran would take his next words, but he needed to say them. He had to know. "Will I be able to call my brother sometimes?" He hadn't found a charger in the bedroom, even though there was electricity in the palace. He hadn't dared asked, either.

Orran nodded. "All right. The queen wants to see you tomorrow."

Blake was nervous again. "What do you think she will say?"

"I don't know, but I told her everything you did, both for Blue and for me. She knows we wouldn't have made it back if you hadn't been there."

Blake hoped it would be enough, but he wouldn't find out until tomorrow, and he knew the waiting would drive him crazy, especially if he had to be alone. "Do you have to go?"

Orran blinked. "Do you want me to go?"

Blake crossed his arms over his chest and huffed. "Why do you always answer a question with another question? No. I don't want you to go. I want you to stay with me until I have to see the queen tomorrow. But I'll understand if you have things to do."

"I can stay."

Blake relaxed. "Good. Can I kiss you now?"

Orran's wide smile was a rare sight, and Blake drank it in. "I thought you'd never ask." Orran paused. "You don't have to ask. I hope you know that. I might not be used to kissing, but it doesn't mean I don't like it."

Blake hadn't been expecting those words, but he was glad he'd heard them. He reached for Orran, and Orran came easily into his arms. Blake was never sure what to expect from him, but it wasn't the pliancy with which Orran allowed him to kiss him. Their lips met, and Blake closed his eyes, overwhelmed. He didn't know how long he and Orran had — if it would be only this night — and he wanted to make the most of it.

He leaned back and looked at Orran. "How much are you ready for?"

Orran seemed dazed, but he answered right away. "Everything. I want everything with you, Blake. I don't care if the others don't understand. I want you."

So they were both aware of how little time they might have. Blake hated this situation, but if he had to leave tomorrow, he wanted to have memories to take with him. He gently moved Orran until his back was to the nest, then he pushed him. Orran stumbled back, his eyes wide. Then he seemed to realize what Blake wanted, and never looking away from him, he lowered himself in the nest.

Blake couldn't breathe, but that didn't stop him from taking off the clothes he'd been given. He abandoned them on the floor, then stepped closer to the nest. He could feel his cheeks heat because of the way Orran was openly staring at his body, but he didn't try to cover himself. Orran had never hidden his body, even though he'd been naked the entire time they'd been together. He wasn't ashamed, and while Blake realized it was because Orran just wasn't used to covering himself, he wanted to be more like him.

He dropped to his knees, and Orran opened his legs. Blake's eyes went wide when he saw what was happening with Orran's groin. "I was right," he said.

Orran frowned. "About what?"

Blake knew his cheeks were bright red as he gestured at Orran's groin. "It's a pouch, and your penis is inside."

"You only now realized it?"

"Hey! I'm human. As you can see, everything is outside for us." Blake bit his lower lip. "So, what now? I'm not sure what to do."

"I'm not, either." Orran reached for Blake. "But I'm sure we can find out together."

Blake decided Orran was right. He needed to stop focusing on their differences and think about all the ways they were similar. They both had a cock, and right now, they were both erect. He reached out tentatively, not wanting to do something wrong or to hurt Orran.

Orran's cock felt like Blake's. The skin was smoother, but the tip glistened with precum, and it jerked when Blake wrapped his hand around it.

It was different, but also familiar, and that helped.

Blake lowered himself on top of Orran. Orran welcomed him, wrapping himself around Blake, holding him close.

Blake let go of Orran's cock to press their bodies closer and sighed in pleasure.

He could move on top of Orran, slide their cocks together. The friction was the same, and he'd always loved frotting. "How is this?" he murmured. He kissed Orran's neck, his collarbone, then licked a path up to his lips.

Orran nodded. His eyes were screwed shut, and while Blake briefly wondered if he was in pain, he could tell that wasn't the case. He'd made sure not to touch Orran's arm, and nothing they were doing should be painful for either of them.

"More," Orran groaned.

Blake wanted to give him the world. He dug his hand into Orran's hair, used the hold to keep his head tilted, and kissed him while he pushed against him. His cock slid, and his eyes went wide as it went *inside*. He froze, not knowing what to do.

Orran opened his eyes. "What's wrong?"

"I don't know if I was supposed to do that."

Orran looked down, even though he couldn't see their groins. "Do what?"

"My cock. It—it slid inside you."

Orran grinned. Blake felt his muscles tighten around his dick, and he almost came. He managed to stop himself by closing his eyes and breathing in and out. When he looked at Orran again, Orran's gaze was soft. "I don't think this is going to be a problem."

"No?" Blake hoped it wouldn't because it felt like heaven.

"No. I'm not fertile right now. You can continue."

Blake blinked. "Fertile?"

"Yes. I won't get pregnant."

Blake opened his mouth, then closed it again. "We'll talk about that later." Once the head of his cock wasn't inside Orran. Blake couldn't even think, let alone wrap his mind around what Orran had just said. "I can continue? Push deeper?"

"Yes."

So Blake did.

He'd had penetrative sex before, and this was similar. Orran felt softer, but he still gripped Blake's cock with his body, and Blake had to focus not to come every time he thrust inside him. Orran seemed to have the same problem, and he clung to Blake's shoulders, pushing toward him and rubbing his cock against him.

It was strange, but in the best of ways.

Orran shuddered in Blake's arms, and Blake felt him come between them. His body contracted around Blake, milking his cock and pushing him to orgasm. He screwed his eyes shut and let the pleasure course through him as he pushed himself deeper. He didn't know if it would hurt Orran, so he did his best to stop moving.

He looked down at Orran to make sure he was okay, and to his relief, Orran was smiling. "Okay?" Blake asked.

Orran nodded. He looked glorious with his hair spread around his face and his flushed cheeks. He was so different from the Orran Blake had met only a week or so ago, and Blake couldn't wait to see what aspect of him he would discover next.

He slowly withdrew from Orran's body, keeping an eye on him. Orran didn't even wince, and when Blake rolled off him and settled next to him, he followed that movement, pressing himself against Blake's side. Blake was surprised, but maybe he shouldn't be.

He wrapped his arm around Orran's shoulders and kissed his temple, enjoying the widening of Orran's eyes. It would take him some time to get used to this kind of affectionate gestures between them, but Blake had nothing but time — or at least, he hoped so.

He cleared his throat. "So. What were you saying about you not being fertile right now?"

CHAPTER TWELVE

Blake couldn't remember if he'd ever been this nervous. He didn't think so. He hadn't had time to be nervous when his parents had kicked him out, and the rest of the time, he didn't care what people thought about him. Today, though, he did. That was why he was nervous — and terrified.

"Stop wiggling so much," Orran said.

He looked nothing like he had when they'd been in Blake's nest only a few hours earlier. There, he'd been wanton. They'd spent the night together, and when they'd woken up this morning, they'd had sex again. Orran was beautiful when he was in the throes of pleasure, and Blake wished he could keep him there forever. Instead, Orran was now perfectly put together, looking like he knew what he was doing.

He probably did.

He'd told Blake the queen wished to see him, and even though Blake wanted to check in on Blue, he wasn't looking forward to it. He might be in prison, but it was a golden prison, and he was more than happy to stay there. He was afraid that once he saw the queen, she would tell him to leave and never come back, and he would lose everything he'd gained this past week.

There was no way out of it, though. The queen reigned over the palace, and since Blake was in it, she reigned over him, too. That meant he had to obey her, and so did Orran.

Orran paused in front of a wide-opened door. "Everything will be okay," he murmured.

Blake shook his head. "How can you know that? What if

she decides to burn me right there in front of you?"

"She won't. That's not the type of person our queen is."

"Maybe, but this is different. This concerns her son. I took care of him, and I don't regret it, but I know he loves me." Probably more than he loved the queen right now since he didn't know her. Blake didn't want the queen to think that he'd been trying to become Blue's father. He'd done what he'd had to do, and he would do it all over again if he had to. Still, it couldn't be an easy thing to accept for the queen.

Orran sighed and took Blake's hand. "I can't promise you'll be allowed to stay. I want you to, and so does the queen, but she isn't the only one who makes decisions. She has a council, and I know she talked to them yesterday. I don't know what decision they made, but we'll have to follow it."

"You think they're going to send me away?"

"I don't know. Most of them trust the queen, and now that her traitor cousin has been arrested, there's no one to whisper in their ears that it's the wrong thing to do. Besides, I know she explained to them what happened and how you kept her son safe."

"None of that is a guarantee I'll be allowed to stay, though."

"It's not. I wish I could tell you that everything will be okay, but I don't know. The clan might not take your presence here well. If they rise against the queen for allowing you to stay, it *will* be a problem."

All of that sounded so complicated. Blake wondered if he *should* stay. He wanted to. He wanted to be with Orran, and that wouldn't be possible if he wasn't allowed to stay. But all of the power stuff was impossible for him to understand. He didn't *want* to understand it. He didn't want anything to do with it.

But he'd saved the queen's son, and this was the result.

"Let's do this," he said, squaring his shoulders.

Orran stared at him for a few moments, then nodded and pulled him into the room.

The queen was inside. She was stretched out on a vast throne that was obviously made for dragons and looked more like a couch, but without the armrests. She wasn't in her dragon form, though. She was in her human one, and she was beautiful.

Blake could guess her dragon form was blue, just like her son's. Her hair was the same color, as were the patches of scales on her skin. It was a lighter blue than Orran's, though, and now that he saw her, Blake saw the color resemblance with Blue.

She stared at Orran and Blake as they walked up to her. Blake swallowed, nervous, at least until a small figure shot from behind the throne and ran to him. Somehow, Blue managed to step onto one of his wings, and he tumbled, rolling on the ground.

Blake rushed over and knelt next to him, gently taking him in his hands. "Are you okay?" he asked, righting the baby.

Blue made a rumbling sound, then, as swiftly as he always did, he climbed on Blake's shoulder and settled there. He rumbled again and rubbed his cheek against Blake's, and Blake couldn't help the way his eyes burned. He wasn't going to cry, but he was damn near doing it. Instead, he gently rubbed the top of Blue's head.

Then he remembered Blue's mother was watching them, and that she might get angry at seeing how familiar her son and Blake were.

Blake wasn't going to put Blue down, though. If this was where Blue wanted to be, then he was allowed. Instead of trying to unhook him, Blake swallowed and looked at his mother. "Your Majesty," he said, awkwardly bowing his head.

He'd asked Orran what he should do or say, but he didn't

remember anything of what Orran had said.

"Welcome," she answered.

"Thank you for everything you did for me."

"I'm sorry you were imprisoned, even if only for one night. I didn't want it to happen, but it had to be done."

"I understand, and I'm not blaming you. I expected a cell, and I got a comfortable bedroom instead." And Orran's presence. Orran had spent the night with Blake, and that meant a lot to him.

"I have a few questions for you," the queen said.

"I'll answer as best as I can."

"Orran told me you took care of my son."

"I did."

"Why? We're dragons. My egg was stolen by humans. Why did you side with us?"

Blake reached up and stroked Blue's tail that hung over his shoulder. "How could I have allowed them to hurt him? Even when he was only an egg, I knew there was a baby inside the shell. I knew what would happen if the people who had stolen him got what they wanted. They would hurt him and possibly kill him. I couldn't allow that to happen, not to him, or to any other dragon."

"You still thought we were animals back then, though."

"I did. It didn't change anything. Even if you were only animals, you don't deserve to be tortured the way you are. You don't deserve to be killed because of what you are."

"So you took my egg and tried to run away with him."

"I did. Then, of course, Orran entered the picture, and you know the rest."

"Why didn't you hand off my son to Orran? They're both dragons."

"Because I didn't know if I could trust him. I know nothing about dragons, Your Majesty. I didn't know if he was a good dragon, not even once I found out he was a shifter. I wasn't about to risk it."

"He could have killed you."

"He could have, but he didn't. He wanted to keep your son safe as much as I did. We worked together, and we brought him home."

She nodded. "I agree. The two of you protected my son as if he were your own. Thank you, both of you. Blue and I are grateful for what you did."

Blake blinked. "You're still calling him Blue?"

She smiled. "I am. It *is* his name, even though it was given to him in an unusual manner. I won't change it. He responds to it, and it fits him."

Blake had been convinced it was a stupid name, but he was glad the queen wasn't changing it. It might have been a bad idea to name him since he wasn't his son, but he couldn't have called Blue *the baby* the entire time. It would have been awkward, especially since Blue wasn't an animal.

"What now?" Orran asked. He took Blake's hand again, and together, they waited for the queen to tell them whether or not Blake would be allowed to say.

She tapped her fingertips on her thigh. "Blue is still young, and as Orran knows, he'll have a tutor."

"Of course," Orran said, sounding confused.

"I want you to retire from the guards and become my son's tutor." She turned her attention to Blake. "I want both of you to tutor him and be his teachers."

It was the last thing Blake had expected. "I'm not a teacher," he said.

"Maybe not, but you love my son. You took care of him when no one else would, and you saved his life, probably more than once. You also saved Orran's life. That means a lot to me, and I want this to happen. I don't know if the humans will ever find out about what we can do, but I want my son to know about them. About you. For so long, we rejected the idea of having any kind of contact with you. We allowed a few bad apples to change the way we saw all of the human race. I now know that that was wrong. There *are* good human beings, as you showed us. I want my son to know that, and I want him to grow up with you by his side. He loves you, and I won't take you away from him."

Blake didn't know what to do. He didn't know what to say. There were a million questions on the tip of his tongue, but he couldn't push any of them out.

"What about your council and the rest of the clan?" Orran asked.

"The council agreed. Some of them didn't like it, but they know it's the right decision. As for the clan, well, I suspect that not everyone will be happy to have Blake with us. As long as they don't hurt him, I won't intervene. But if anyone hurts you in any way, Blake, I want you to come to me. I am the queen. They need to respect me and my decisions, and I want to know immediately when they don't."

Blake nodded. He still couldn't say anything. His life had changed in the past week and a half, and he felt lost.

But he wasn't going anywhere. He was staying at the palace with Blue and Orran. He might not have any idea what was next, but he did know that this was the beginning of a new chapter of his life. He had love. He had a family.

What more could he want?

YOU MAY ALSO ENJOY THE FOLLOWING FROM EXTASY BOOKS INC:

Air and Earth
Catherine Lievens

Excerpt

Henry stayed strong until he left Edward's hospital room. Then, his knees buckled, and he was flooded with pain, fear, and anger. He reached out, needing to hold himself up, but before he could touch the wall, Alcott was there. He took Henry by the arm and guided him toward the chairs that lined the wall. Henry was grateful, and he smiled at Alcott, but he didn't know if that smile was a real one or looked more like a grimace. He hoped Alcott would understand either way.

"I can believe Lyle did that," he murmured.

"I'm sorry," Alcott murmured back. They looked at each other, with Alcott standing over Henry, Henry sitting in the hard plastic chair. Henry didn't know what to do. He wanted to go find Lyle and make sure he paid for what he did to Edward.

He'd hurt Edward. He'd left him for dead. He would have killed Edward if Edward hadn't managed to escape. He needed to pay for that, but how? They couldn't go to the police and explain what had happened. Humans didn't know about element wielders, and it had to stay that way. What was going to happen to Lyle, then? Would he be released?

Henry wouldn't allow that to happen. He couldn't. "I want to talk to Lyle."

Alcott jerked back. "You can't."

"Why not?"

"You shouldn't see him. You already know what he did and why he did it. Why do you want to talk to him?"

"I just need to face him." Even though Henry knew Lyle had done it because he was with Purity, he needed more. Lyle had always been a friend, Henry's best friend. How could he have changed so much that he hadn't hesitated to attack Edward? Lyle and Edward weren't friends, not the way Lyle and Henry had been, but they'd been close. Why had Lyle attacked Edward? Why did he think elements should stick with each other? Edward had already explained Lyle felt he deserved more than the job he had with the company, but Henry had a hard time believing that. He needed to ask Lyle, and hopefully, Lyle would answer.

But more than that, Henry wanted to get his hands on Lyle and hurt him the way he'd hurt Edward.

A hand on Henry's shoulders made him jerk. He looked up to see Alcott, his hands raised as if he was trying to make Henry see he wasn't going to hurt him. Henry realized he wasn't acting normally, and he tried to relax. Alcott was no doubt worried, and Henry didn't want him to be.

"I don't think it's a good idea," Alcott said slowly.

Henry shook his head. "I don't care. I need to talk to him."

"You have nothing to say to him, and I don't think he has anything to say to you."

Henry shook his head and rose to his feet. He felt better now, and he was thankful for the moment of reprieve, but he did need to see Lyle. "What would you do if your best friend did what Lyle did? If he attacked your brother, left him for dead? If he'd been working against you the entire time and you hadn't suspected?"

Alcott hesitated, and Henry knew he had him. They were friends, and Henry knew him better than he knew himself some days. He could tell how Alcott would react, what he was thinking about — how to keep Henry safe without stifling him. Alcott was quiet, and he'd done his best to stay just a bodyguard since he'd started working with Henry, but he was failing.

Henry couldn't say he minded. He needed a friend more than a bodyguard right now.

Alcott sighed. "Fine. I see what you mean. If my best friend did something like that, I would go find him, too. But you're not me, Henry. You don't have to see him. There's no reason for you to."

"I still like to, though. Please." Alcott stared at Henry, and Henry held his breath. He'd found early on that if he said please, Alcott would be more inclined to do what he wanted. He didn't know why that was, and he didn't want to analyze it right now. He just knew that Alcott was weak when it came to politeness, and he was going to use it if he had to.

Alcott finally sighed. "Fine. Let me call the warehouse. I'll ask them to get him ready so you can see him. But it's the one and only time you do this, understood? I understand you want closure, but it's all this can be. You want answers from him, but you can't hurt him, no matter how much you wish to."

Edward nodded curtly. It was true that he wanted to hurt Lyle, but he knew better. He didn't know who was going to make Lyle pay, but he suspected Dakota wouldn't hesitate to take the situation in hand. If he didn't, well, Henry would find a way. He was going to avenge his brother, and he was going to find out who was behind Purity. Lyle had to know something.

He was done with anonymous notes, with people threatening him and his brother and his company for making good business deals. He was done with all of this. He didn't care who was behind Purity and what they wanted. They needed to leave him alone.

Alcott stepped away, but he didn't move far. He kept an eye on Henry as he took his phone out, and Henry stayed right where he was. Alcott was his bodyguard, and he always kept an eye on him. In the beginning, it had been irritating. Now, it was something else.

"What are you two up to?" Dakota asked, making Henry jump.

His heart raced, and he pressed a hand against it. "I didn't hear you," he explained when he noticed Dakota's bemused expression.

"That's what I thought. Which means you're doing something you shouldn't be doing."

Henry straightened his back. Dakota wasn't his boss, and he couldn't make any kind of decision when it came to him. "I want to see Lyle, and Alcott is calling the place where he's being kept."

Dakota grimaced. "That's what I thought. I'd ask why you want to talk to him, but I understand. I'd want the same if he'd done what he did to me. Besides, he hurt Bay's mate, and that's enough for me."

"Do you know why he did it?" Dakota arched a brow, and Henry continued, "I know he said he felt he deserved a bigger role in the company, but that can't be right. He was my best friend, but he wasn't part of the family. Why should my father have given him part of the company?"

Dakota shook his head. "You know him better than I do. I can only tell you what he told Bay and me."

"That's why I want to talk to him. It doesn't make sense."

"If I had to guess, I'd say Purity probably put him against you. Even if he was only slightly resentful, they would have realized that, and they would have used it against him and you."

It made sense, no matter how little Henry liked it. Lyle had been his friend, but it was true that he was easily influenced.

"I just can't believe he did this."

"I'm sorry for your loss. But you still have Edward, and you have us now, too."

Henry nodded, but it wasn't the same thing. He still had his brother, that much was true. Lyle had been his friends for years, though. It was like losing another piece of himself after already losing so much. Both his parents were dead, and the only family he had was Edward and their grandfather, who detested them. Lyle had been part of Henry's family, and now, he wasn't anymore, and in the worst of ways.

"Everything is set," Alcott said as he came back. His gaze flicked to Dakota, but he turned his attention back to Henry. "We can go whenever you want."

"Now."

Alcott looked at Dakota again, and Dakota sighed and nodded. "You can take him. I'm going to hang around a little more to make sure everything is set here. Then I'll join you unless you're already done and back home. Don't worry about me." He turned to Henry. "If you have any questions, feel free to call me. I'll answer if I can."

Henry nodded, but he was already focused on what was going to happen now. He didn't know what he would say to Lyle, if he would try to hit him or hurt him. He didn't know anything right now. His life felt like it had imploded, and he didn't know how to deal with it.

"Are you okay?" Alcott asked as they walked away.

"I don't know. I don't know anything right now," Henry answered. If there was one person he could be honest with when it came to this, it was Alcott.

****

Alcott was worried about Henry. He was always worried about Henry, which was his job, but he knew there was more to it. He couldn't think about that right now, though. Henry was about to face his best friend — former best friend — a man who had almost killed Henry's brother. If Alcott knew one thing about Henry, it was how much Edward meant to him. It wasn't going to end well, and Alcott didn't know what to do. He could have stopped it, made sure Henry never talked to Lyle, but he knew it wasn't possible. It wasn't because technically, Henry was his boss right now. It was because he knew Henry would torture himself if he couldn't get answers. Hopefully, he would, but Alcott wouldn't put it past Lyle to string him around. If it meant he made it out of this alive, Lyle would do just about anything.

Alcott glanced at Henry, who was sitting next to him in the car. They were almost there, and Henry hadn't said a word since they left the hospital. He was probably still worried about Edward, and Alcott didn't blame him. Seeing Edward in the hospital bed had shaken him, too. He'd realized he was starting to care for the two brothers even before it happened, but what had happened to Edward had solidified that. Edward wasn't just a client. He was Bay's mate, and Bay one was of one of Alcott's best friends. That made Edward family, and since Henry was his brother, it made him family, too.

Alcott shouldn't be as thrilled as he was by that.

"We're there," he murmured as he steered the car into the parking lot.

Henry leaned forward and looked at the warehouse. "It doesn't look like much," he commented.

That got a chuckle out of Alcott. "I realize that. It is something, though. It looks this way on purpose so that people won't realize what happens inside."

Edward looked at him. "And what happens inside?"

"I don't know what you're thinking, but it's probably not that. This is the place where Dakota trains us. He makes sure we know how to do your job. It's also the place where some of us live."

Henry blinked. "Do you live here?"

So far, Alcott had been staying in Henry's apartment. He was Henry's bodyguard, and he had to keep close. "Yes.

When I'm not on a job, I live here."

Henry wrinkled his nose, and Alcott had to look away. He didn't want to find Henry adorable. "Don't you want your own place, maybe an apartment? Isn't this crowded?"

"A bit, but it's what I need." Because Alcott didn't have a blood family, and these people, the people who lived there with him, who worked with him, were his family. He might not like all of them, but with most, he'd become friends, and he was comfortable sharing a living space with them.

He parked in front of the warehouse and looked at Edward. "You don't have to do this," he repeated.

Henry's expression became serious again. "I have to do it."

Alcott sighed. "I had to try."

"I know, and I thank you for that. But I truly have to do this. I need to ask him why."

"You realize he probably won't have an answer for you."

"I know. I'll deal with that if it happens. I still need to face him. He almost killed my brother, and I will never forgive him for that."

"You don't have to forgive him. I hate that you're going through this, that you're losing someone you're so close to."

Henry shook his head. "I've already lost him. I just want to know why."

They exited the car, and Henry followed Alcott inside. Alcott had made sure everyone knew they were coming, so they didn't even have to stop on their way to Lyle's cell. Henry looked around curiously, but he didn't ask questions, and Alcott was grateful. He was tense. He didn't like what was happening, even though he knew he couldn't stop it. He didn't want Henry to get hurt more than he already was. He had to protect him because it was his job.

And because he loved him.

He nodded at the guard who was sitting in the small room before the hallway where the cells were located, and Mercer nodded back. He didn't say anything, didn't try to talk to Alcott, and Alcott was relieved. The sooner they did this, the sooner they would be out of here, and that was what he wanted. He wanted to take Henry home to the apartment, to make sure he was okay, to make sure he rested and took time to grieve. No matter how angry Henry was, he was still losing a lot today. Lyle was his best friend, one of the few people he was close to.

Alcott wanted to get his hands on Lyle and strangle him himself for what he'd done.

Instead, he guided Henry to the cell Lyle was in. It wasn't hard to understand which one it was because Lyle was yelling, screaming at someone to let him out, telling anyone who'd listen that his lawyer was going to hear about this.

Alcott almost snorted. He managed to keep the sound in, but he didn't miss the amused glance Henry gave him. Then Henry shook his head and stopped in front of the cell, and Lyle suddenly shut up. He peered through the bars at the small window, and his eyes widened when he saw Henry there. "Henry. Thank God. You're here to get me out."

Henry took a step back. He looked outraged, but just like always, he took a moment to gather his thoughts, and when he spoke, his voice was cold and calm. "Take you out? Why should I do that?"

"You don't understand. I had nothing to do with what happened to Edward. I promise. I said those things because that man was threatening me, but you know I wouldn't hurt Edward."

"It's not what Edward said."

Lyle paled so much that Alcott wondered if he was about to faint. "Edward?"

"We found him. My brother is strong, stronger than you thought. He managed to get out of the place where you kept him, and he's in the hospital." Henry moved closer. "He's in the hospital because you hurt him."

Lyle loudly swallowed. "I'm sorry," he started.

Henry shook his head. "I don't care. Why did you hurt my brother? Why do you work for Purity? You never thought elements shouldn't mix."

Lyle hesitated, but he probably knew he wouldn't get out of it. Henry wanted answers, but he wouldn't compromise to get them.

"I was promised a higher spot in the company."

Henry blinked. "Higher spot? You already have one of the highest-paying jobs. What more did you want?" Henry paused, and his mouth slightly opened as he realized what was happening. "You want to be vice president. You want Edward's job."

"He doesn't want it anyway. You know he doesn't like to be vice president."

"I don't care what he likes or doesn't like. Being the vice president is his job, and it won't change. He's my brother."

"I'm your best friend."

Henry rushed toward the door and tried to hook a hand in between the bars and snatch Lyle. Alcott had expected it, though, and he grabbed Henry's waist, pulling him back against his chest. "It's not worth it," he murmured in Henry's ear. "Don't hurt him. It's not worth it."

Henry wiggled. "It would be worth it to feel his blood on my hands."

It wasn't Henry talking. It was the pain, the fury, and Alcott knew Henry would be grateful that he hadn't let him do this. He held onto him, keeping him against his chest until he finally stopped moving. Then, he held him some more.

Henry finally nodded. "I'm fine," he said.

"You're sure?"

"I'm sure."

Alcott let him go. Henry stepped closer, but Lyle had finally understood what was happening, and he wasn't near the door anymore. Henry peeked inside. "Why?"

"I already told you why. Please, Henry. I know it was stupid. I know I shouldn't have done this. But I've been working for you and your father for so long. I deserved more than I got. I'm your best friend. I'm family."

Henry made a disgusted sound and shook his head. "As of now, you're nothing. I won't ever see you again. I don't care what you have to say to me or what you try to use as a bargaining chip. I don't care. You're dead to me, Lyle."

Henry turned around. He walked away, ignoring Lyle's screams and his begging, and Alcott followed him, not giving Lyle a second glance. As far as he was concerned, the man was dead to him, too.

About the Author

Catherine is the creator of several series, most of them paranormal, including the Whitedell Pride Series and the Gillham Pack Series. While she graduated in translation, she decided to go the writer's way because it was more fun to create her own stories and characters.

She's been living in Italy for more than twenty years, but she's a daughter of the North—Belgium to be precise—and she misses it so much that she's already planning to move back.

She loves pizza—probably too much—her son, her pets, and of course, books. She sneaks some reading time into her schedule every time she has five minutes free from writing, demands from her various pets and son, and lastly, housework.

Connect with her:

lievens.catherine@gmail.com
BookBub: https://www.bookbub.com/authors/catherine-lievens
Website: https://authorcatherinelievens.com/
Facebook: https://www.facebook.com/catherine.lievens.9
Facebook Group: https://www.facebook.com/groups/411788002341528/
Twitter: https://twitter.com/authorCLievens
Newsletter: http://eepurl.com/c-uvKn